W9-BHB-318

G

A STREET STORY

PANTHEON BOOKS   NEW YORK

COPYRIGHT © 1999 BY JOHN BERGER

All rights reserved under International and Pan-American Copyright Conventions. Published in the United States by Pantheon Books, a division of Random House, Inc., New York, and simultaneously in Canada by Random House of Canada Limited, Toronto.

Pantheon Books and colophon are registered trademarks of Random House, Inc.

Library of Congress Cataloging-in-Publication Data

Berger, John.
  King : a street story / John Berger.
    p. cm.
  ISBN 0-375-40556-9
  1. Dogs—Fiction. I. Title.
PR6052.E564K56 1999
823'.914—dc21   98-44838   CIP

Random House Web Address: www.randomhouse.com

BOOK DESIGN BY MIA RISBERG

Printed in the United States of America
First Edition *Bt   20 00//1 00   5/99*
9 8 7 6 5 4 3 2 1

y un horizonte de perros
ladra muy lejos del río

—FEDERICO GARCÍA LORCA

6:00 A.M.

I am mad to try. I hear these words in my sleep, and when I hear them I coo like a pigeon somewhere at the back of my throat, where the gullet joins the nose. The part which goes dry when you are frightened. I am mad to try to lead you to where we live.

The M.1000 runs north out of the city. There's traffic day and night, nonstop, except when there's an accident, or when strikers put up a barricade. Twelve kilometres from the city centre and four from the sea there is a zone where people never stop unless obliged. Not because it's dangerous but because it has been forgotten. Even those who do stop for a moment forget it immediately afterwards. It's empty, yet it is large. It would take half an hour to run round it, trotting fast. There's talk of building a stadium, the biggest ever, to hold a hundred thousand spectators. In the next century the Olympic Games could be held there. Others argue that since the main airport is to the east of the city it would make more sense to build a stadium in the east. The speculators, Vico says, are placing bets on both sites. Ours is called Saint Valéry, and that's where we are going.

The traffic on the M.1000 can be killing. I keep to the hard shoulder. We only have to go as far as the Elf filling station, where it smells of high octane—a little like the smell of diamonds. You have never smelt diamonds?

A month ago a gang of kids poured petrol over an old man who was sleeping in a street behind the Central Station and then they threw a match onto him. He woke up in flames.

A heretic's death.

What the hell do you mean? The poor sod didn't know one church from another.

Maybe his heresy was to have no money?

When we get to the gas station we go down the slope, onto the wasteland where one day there may be an Olympic stadium. There are no words for what makes up the wasteland because everything on it is smashed and has been thrown away, and for most fragments there are no proper names.

The winter is over and it's spring. The nights are still cold enough to make a body shiver if it's not well covered, but no longer cold enough to kill. It's good, isn't it, to have lived to see another spring. Everything's coming into leaf. Vica's radishes are coming up well. The plastic sheet Vico spread over them helped, but what made the real difference was the soil we stole. Vica is called Vica because she lives with Vico.

The terrain is used as a dump. Smashed lorries. Old boilers. Broken washing machines. Rotary lawn mowers. Refrigerators which don't make cold any more. Wash basins which are cracked. There are also bushes and small trees and tough flowers like pheasant's-eye and viper's-grass.

This is what I call my mountain. When they destroyed the old building here thirty years ago, they used a swinging weight and cable. It wasn't crushed, it was knocked over. So the scrap mountain is easy to climb.

At the top I systematically bark. Afterwards the other sounds become clearer: some kids shouting towards Ardeatina Street, a sparrow warning other sparrows about a crow, a train on the tracks to the north, faintly a ship's siren, and, behind everything, the howl from the M.1000.

All dogs dream of forests, whether they've ever been in one or not. Even Egyptian dogs dream of forests.

The street I was born in smelt of sawmills. They brought whole trees to the mills, their bark already stripped off their trunks, glistening on ten-wheel lorries.

My first schooling was on the banks of a river where they loaded gravel into barges. A great river and, like any other, a flowing demonstration of pure indifference. I saw it carry away three children in one night.

In the forest I was carefree. I followed trails wherever they led, I ran between pines as tall as churches and jumped the bars of shadow, and when I was panting, I lolloped to the forest edge, where the girls spied and waited for men, and there I lay down on the grass.

When the sun set, the forest was filled with blackness, not with the colour black but the mystery, the invitation of black. Blackness as in a black coat, as in black hair, as in a touching you didn't know existed.

Although Vica is not with me, I hear her voice—this happens often.

King, keep your mouth shut, she hisses, you don't know what you're talking about!

I'm talking about sex.

On the street there's rape, nothing else, she says.

Vica and Vico have an overcoat which hangs over the foot of their bed. At night, if either of them has to go out, they put it on. On her it looks big. On him you think the coat is going out to shit by itself; it hides him entirely. It's lined with sheep-skin, and its colour is a dirty white, like snow after they've put salt down.

Vico says coats like this were once standard issue for the Swedish army. It keeps a man warm when the temperature is minus 40. He says he should know because his factory was approached about manufacturing them.

I'm not sure. When people here talk about the past, they tend to exaggerate, because sometimes the exaggerations too help to keep them a little warmer.

From the scrap mountain I survey the whole of Saint Valéry. I know these living quarters as a man knows something he wears. Saint Valéry is laid out on the ground like their sheepskin coat. We live in the coat of Saint Valéry. In the winter it saves us dying from hypothermia. And in the summer heat it hides us when we undress and wash.

The Vicos live in the cuff of the right sleeve, and an elder tree grows more or less where the sleeve buttons would be. Jack lives up in the collar. Jack is the only inhabitant of Saint Valéry who has floorboards and a proper gutter system. He was the first inhabitant, and he never gets wet. Nobody can settle here without his agreement, and he charges everyone a rent for the land. Vica cooks for him once or twice a week and that's our rent. Marcello, who works on Sunday cleaning out tanker lorries, supplies him with a full gas cylinder whenever he needs one. His house has not only floorboards but a wattle roof and a front door which can really be locked. If you wanted to break in there, the easiest way would be to open a window; his windows, unlike ours, open.

The poor steal from each other the same as the rich do. The poor usually do it without any calculation, their thefts aren't planned. Every day the poor imagine their luck changing. They don't believe it will ever change, but they can't stop picturing to themselves what would happen if it did. And they don't want to miss the moment should it come. When they spot a cigarette lighter on the ground beside a pair of shoes, they grab it, as if Chance herself had given it to them. And they say to themselves, Here is the sign our luck has changed. When they grab what they spot, they don't think Theft. They think Luck. No, the poor don't plan the damage they do beforehand. They don't make notes of every detail whilst drinking from a crystal glass and checking the time in Tokyo. The poor decide at the last minute.

You talk too much! Vica shouts, although she is not here. You talk too much, King, you don't know anything!

Around the back of the collar lives Anna. The concrete block-house was always there, maybe it once housed an electrical trans-former. It has no window. Anna moved in without asking Jack. She came by night, and by the time day broke, she had already installed herself. Jack walked over to confront her.

You take your fucking chin out of here! she said, I don't play your game.

You will, said Jack.

I haven't built a thing, she said, I'm not on your housing estate.

If you don't want to get smoked out, dear lady—

Dear lady! I'll give you dear lady. And she picked up a beer can and threw it at him.

He adjusted his immense shoulders.

I'll be carrying you off in ten minutes, he said, you'd better get your things together.

And of course she started to pay him. Six cans of beer a week.

Here, he told her, there's no mucking about. Understand?

Jack doesn't believe anything can make the world better than it is, yet he insists on no mucking about. This is the only law in Saint Valéry. Jack's Law. And it's why he spends hours sewing himself jackets made from the pages of flower catalogs. Maybe that's difficult to grasp; in the coat there are many things to understand without knowing why.

In the left cuff lives Joachim. His place is covered with a giant lorry tarpaulin. Vico would correct me and point out that it's polyamide. Underneath, Joachim has arranged windows and a door. He's the biggest man in Saint Valéry, he has a beard and his body is very hairy. He listens a lot to the radio, he has a large one with flashing lights of which he's very proud, and he has a cat called Catastrophe. On his chest is a tattoo of a woman with bare breasts, and under it, in red and blue letters, the name EVA. He's a good friend of Marcello's, and on long summer evenings they play dice together. Vica believes he was a sailor. Vico says, Never, he's too big, sailors are never that big. Joachim talks a lot to Catastrophe, in the tone of voice a man usually reserves for chatting up women.

At night, Joachim told me, when Catastrophe lies with me, she purrs, which is more than you do, King, you with your fucking fidelity.

Malak lives under the right arm. She's here thanks to Liberto. He answers for her, and he never touches her. Somehow their paths must have crossed. He is old enough to be her father as well as her rescuer.

Once I heard her say to him, Come and die with me!

Liberto drew himself up as only a short Spaniard can and said, You will never insult me or yourself again like that, Malak. Never.

Liberto has a wound which won't heal above his left eye and a mustache of soft black hair. He has been in prison several times and he's the only one here who reads books.

Saul reads the Bible, and Vico has read thousands of books in his life, and here he reads no more. To read, a man needs to love himself, not much but a little. And Vico doesn't.

In the left pocket lives Danny. His place is a wrecked container and he heats it with a brazier when it's freezing. His hands are always warm and he has the pointed face of a fell hound. His nose and mouth have been hurt many times—although he can't be more than twenty.

To start his day, Danny needs to hear laughter, as others need a mug of coffee and a chunk of toast with hot margarine.

Some girls, he jokes, are like wildflowers, they grow wild in the woods!

Everyone has invented a toaster to put on their gas ring. Vico made his from a car radio. Marcello repeats again and again he's going to steal electricity from one of the cables which cross the terrain, though he hasn't brought it off yet. Danny is the only one who doesn't have a toaster. Instead he uses a joke.

Before the end of the year, he says, I'm going to find an American Express woman who will fall in love with me. Old enough to be your aunt? asks Joachim. No, replies Danny, my age! She's a dwarf with hair on her chin! insists Joachim. She's beautiful, says Danny, as beautiful as a mink and every morning we'll take breakfast in the Bella Venezia! Why not in bed? asks Corinna, who speaks so rarely. Because, says Danny, she likes to fuck all night and get up early! We go to the Bella Venezia and she takes hot chocolate!

The shack over there near the left shoulder was built by Luc, who has gone.

Me, I run to places where there's no fear, I told Luc one day.

There's fear everywhere, he said.

Not where I go.

Where there's life, there's fear, he repeated.

In these places there's death, I told him, there's fighting for life, there's hiding, there's running away, there's being hungry, and there's no fear.

What makes a dog run away, then?

The desire to live.

KING

You've never seen a dog trembling?

A dog trembles when he doesn't know what to do.

Like us!

No, you tremble when you know what to do as much as when you don't!

Fart off, dog.

I said nothing. I just looked at him. What a fuck-up, King, he said. They've lent you to me, and do you know why they've done that? They don't say, but they've lent you to me so I don't try it again.

He pushed with his nose and rubbed it up and down between my eyes.

Luc's mouth is a little to the side of where it should be. Everything he says is an attempt to shift it back to its proper place. His tongue pushes from the corner of his mouth as he talks. Sometimes from the left, sometimes from the right, what he is saying matters less than this constant effort to shift his mouth.

They reckon they're doing it for the best, he said, yet they can't tell what's going on in here, can they? And he banged his forehead against mine.

When he tried he had broken his left wrist. It's bandaged now and still pains him.

Where I'm not human at all is that I'm possessive about pain. I mean the pain of others. The pain in Luc's hand, for instance. I take over the one who is suffering, and I growl if anybody approaches. It is something I learnt from my mother, and now it's stronger than me.

Luc, I tell him, let's go and get something to eat.

You and I, we're going to eat meat tonight! he replies. Do what I tell you.

We set off downtown, for the Quirina area. We chose the butcher shop carefully. A small one with only one man serving. Before going in, Luc arranged his coat like a cape, attached at the neck and without his arms in the sleeves. I stayed outside.

Luc enters and asks the butcher whether he has any oxtail to make ossobuco, a dish to last for several days. I need good meat, he adds, and he holds up his bandaged arm.

An accident? asks the butcher.

No, bitten by a dog.

This is my cue to push open the door and go in. Which is what I do.

Is he your dog? asks the butcher.

Never seen him, says Luc, but if I were you I'd get rid of him, he doesn't look right to me.

KING

Out! shouts the butcher.

I take another step forward.

What about a bucket of water, if you've got one in the back? Luc suggests.

Don't go near him, whispers the butcher and goes out by the back door.

I growl.

Luc, with considerable dexterity, picks up from the counter with his right hand a two- or three-kilo cut of prepared roast beef, laced with string and pork fat, and slides it under his cape.

I could have gone at this moment, slunk away. Something prevented me; I wanted to make a point for Luc to see and take in. I wanted to say something about withstanding the shit, about pride. So I stood there, raised my head, and bared my teeth.

The butcher flings the water over the counter onto me. It all lands on me. He must be used to sluicing down. Not every man can aim water.

I stand there dripping. And I hope he doesn't see my flanks trembling.

Strange dog, says Luc, I've never seen one like him before.

Slowly I back away, step by step, reach the door, and disappear.

Your meat is kosher, isn't it? Luc is meant to ask now.

Why the hell should it be kosher? the butcher will demand, puzzled.

Je suis désolé, I thought it was a kosher butcher shop. Désolé.

Back in the Rancho, Luc straightaway cooked the meat in his oven. On feast days, if somebody in Saint Valéry has enough to share, they invite their favourite neighbours. On an ordinary day, if by some good fortune somebody has found more than enough, they keep it to themselves. Luc and I finished the meat between us.

Then, replete, we lay on a blanket and watched the headlights of the stream of vehicles coming south towards us on the M.1000. And sometimes we glanced at the taillights, like pinheads of blood, of the vehicles going away.

Seven weeks later Luc killed himself. The second time he didn't bungle it. He jumped from a bridge.

Now that he is dead, I want to show Luc a wall I remember where mushrooms grow in the spring. Hidden in the grass they are black and cool like a black nose pointing at the sky. They smell of earth and the breath of old women who tell fortunes for a bar of black chocolate. Luc will find a kilo of morels there. And we'll cook them together with parsley and garlic and then make an omelette with four eggs and a tablespoon of white wine to make it light, and we'll halve the omelette between us. The dead man and the dog.

KING

Saul, who used to live under the ground in what was once a basement in the left bottom hem of the coat, has already taken over Luc's Rancho. With Jack's permission, of course.

Saul, who is as old as Vico, wears a tweed cap at all times. I've never seen him without it. Marcello gave Saul a TV, which he uses to sit on. He speaks only about once a week. He worked for twenty years in an abattoir and there was some scandal, for which he was sacked. To me he has said several times: When I was young I used to go ferreting for rabbits! Do you want to come? As soon as he has a spare moment he reads the Bible. He holds the book in his open hands like a bird who has just alighted. And his faith is so intense that his eyes close in belief as he reads.

A little to the southeast of the coat, in the direction of the shortcut to the sea which avoids the city, there is a hollow in the earth, a long shallow hole. Perhaps it was once part of an underground tunnel which fell in. It is not dangerous because its sides are not steep. Numerous homeless lovers have discovered that at night this crater offers a kind of shelter. Danny calls it the Boeing. It's more or less the shape and size of a jet airliner, and he found down there in the muck a battered suitcase with an airline label for Houston still attached to it. Then he made one of his jokes:

I wouldn't say this Boeing 747 is flying blind, but I've just been to look and the instrument panel in the pilot's cabin is in Braille!

Corinna lives in a van near the inside pocket. She gets smaller every day, she's withdrawing from her skin.

Lazy-good-for-nothing! she calls me.

I guard the place, I tell her.

If we all guarded, there'd be nothing to guard.

There isn't much, I said.

Look at my hands and what have I to show? she asked.

Your hands, I said.

She pretends to kick me with one of her men's boots and spits. After she has smiled, Corinna always spits; it's to do with her lack of teeth.

After Vico and Vica built the Hut, it took Corinna two months before she acknowledged them. Her van is less than a stone's throw away. For two months she pretended to be deaf whenever Vico or Vica addressed her. Then one bright morning she said to Vica:

If you want a longer clothesline, you can tie it here to the mirror on my van. Washing on the line has never frightened me.

Alfonso is the richest man in Saint Valéry, and he lives in the right pocket, opposite to where Saul lived before Saul moved into Luc's place. Alfonso built a wooden lean-to, against a brick wall which had been left standing. He did all the woodwork himself. His place has a tiled roof and a chimney pipe which goes through it, and a wooden doorstep. On the doorstep he sometimes leaves something for me, but not this morning.

KING

He's the richest inhabitant because he can sing. He takes his electric guitar and sings in the metro. Once he took me with him. His idea was that I should collect the money whilst he went on playing, and that is what I did. Then he met up with a cutty sark and he decided she could do it better than me. She could. But she forced him to let her keep most of the money for herself. So he was the loser.

He has a beautiful voice, and it's a loser's voice, which the best male voices often are. Alfonso's trouble is that he loses too much. He spends everything he gets on cutty sarks. He brings them back for the night. They leave early, they take his money, and the next day he doesn't go out, he stays indoors, getting his sad voice back. According to Vica he has no brain at all, less than a cock's, she says.

Here is Marcello's favourite spot for sunning himself. I don't know where Marcello goes in winter, he left in October. According to Jack he should arrive in March and he hasn't arrived yet. He collects electrical appliances; the whole left sleeve is full of them. Five TVs, big ones. He talks a lot about stealing electricity for himself and the rest of us, he says it would be simple. Nothing, says Liberto, is ever simple. When it's sunny, Marcello takes everything off except his shorts and lies in the sun. There's a patch of grass and a bush which shelter you. Marcello says things started to go wrong when the wife left him. Men who have just been abandoned have a special smell, quite distinct from those who live alone. A smell not so different from sour milk. He worked in the steel industry. Do you have children? Vica once asked him. He nodded and opened another can of beer. I ask myself whether Marcello and his short fringe—he has sandy hair—and his soft mouth and his young terrier eyes, I ask myself whether he too has gone for good.

You want to know how I ended up in Saint Valéry? I walked. Along the roads. Walking on the left so I faced the oncoming traffic. I had no clear idea about what I was looking for, I simply imagined things being better by the sea. It took me forty-nine days. Mostly I slept by day and walked by night.

Why I left my home is a different question, and I'm not sure of the answer. By which I mean I don't know exactly what happened. Everybody here will tell you the same thing. Suddenly there is no in and no out, and you have to survive the next hour alone, and the next and the next and the next. Nobody sees it coming when it comes. For each of us it came differently. And for all of us it happened when we weren't looking. I heard it before I saw it. The noise of traffic which stays still. Later there is the smell of urine.

When I at last arrived in this city, Vico spotted me under the abandoned cranes down by the B.9 docks. He was on his way to the new port where the yachts tie up. He hoped to find one flying an Italian flag, because he originally came from Naples. In those days he still believed there was a slim chance he would find a temporary job if he took initiatives. So he proposed himself to the yacht owners as a guide for the Aegean!

He didn't any longer know what he looked like. He had combed his hair, found a razor and shaved, brushed his trousers, wiped his shoes, cleaned his nails, and after all this, he didn't see his own disarray.

He looked inexplicable. Like we all do. It is visible under our cheekbones, in the way the skin is pulled around our mouths and the way our shoulders hunch.

We don't need a guide, the yachtsman tells him.

KING

Both history and geography are my subject, promises Vico.

His voice is surprising, as it is both light and delicate. It poses on a sentence like a butterfly on a flower, wings upright and fluttering.

We could do with a stripper, and that's something, old man, I don't think you can find for us! says the yachtsman and they all laugh.

The hatred which the strong feel for the weak as soon as the weak get too close is particularly human; it doesn't happen with animals. With humans there is a distance which must be respected, and when it isn't, it is the strong, not the weak, who feel affronted, and from the affront comes hatred. Feeling this hatred coming from the yachtsmen, I growled.

One of them, wearing a pair of bronze sunglasses, looked over his shoulder and said, Push off, dog!

I know places off the map! insisted Vico in his butterfly voice.

We don't need your dog, your map, or you, is that clear?

He's not my dog.

Just stop blocking the view, will you?

They turned their backs and walked away.

What happened to you? is the first thing Vico asks me. Where are you from?

I stare at him.

Then let me introduce myself, he says. I'm called Vico. I'm a descendant of the great Giambattista. I had my own factory, that's true for certain. A small factory and my neighbours were Philips, they were good neighbours.

Shit! I say. What did you make?

We made clothes, working clothes. Polyester, polycarbamide, elasthanne, polytetrafluorethylene, vinyl . . .

Every name sounds like a flower, and the butterfly's wings flutter in his voice as he pronounces them.

I look at him. He has grey hair and a forehead with many lines running across it. He's in his mid-sixties. Maybe older, for he has enormous ears, and ears enlarge with age. He has ears like an elephant, with hairs growing out of them. He has dark eyes. Each one like a black stone in a paw print made in sand still wet from the sea. The stones keep very still. His hands, with their thin, cracked fingernails, are small and delicate, like a girl's. Yet covered with calluses and grey—as if he had been working for years with lead or some other metal. If you saw only his hands, you'd say the hands of an acetylene welder's daughter who took over her father's job when his eyes gave out!

We made blouses, trousers, capes, caps, and our great speciality was gloves, he told me. We made the best insulated gloves in Europe, using a derivative of quartz. What's your name?

I wasn't going to tell him immediately.

KING

I'll call you King, he said.

After walking awhile, he sat on the edge of a fountain in a square and pulled out a tin of Fanta from the plastic bag he was carrying. He opened it and held it out to me. I shook my head.

Something changes, he said, around the age of five. In peacetime, of course. If one is thinking of a period of war everything is different. In war there is no childhood, let's be clear, King, no childhood. Until the age of five, in peacetime, the unexpected comes as a surprise, and surprises up to the age of five are usually good. Then something alters and the unexpected is invariably bad. Very bad. Take me, now. I wrap myself up from head to foot as a protection against the cold and against the unexpected. I try to keep them out day and night. The cold and the unexpected. Would you care to see where I sleep?

I'd never before heard a man talk like this, and I went along and he showed me where he slept underneath the Sublicius Bridge. He gave me bread soaked in milk. Vica wasn't with him then. It was a month before he even mentioned Vica to me. One day she showed up.

He's my dog! she said immediately when she saw me, come here, my pet.

7:30 A.M.

Over there Vica is relieving herself as she does every morning behind the tyres. Vica, like I told you, is Vico's wife. When a woman has so little privacy, it's good at certain moments if a small curtain can be made for her with words. So I'll tell the story about the swallow.

The bird flies by mistake into a room. It circles and cannot find the open window it came in by. Repeatedly, it tries to fly through the windowpanes into the sky it can still see. It beats its wings more and more frantically and they make the noise of a wooden rattle—one of those with a handle which you twirl. The bird does not believe in the glass. It thinks itself in the sky but

29

discovers it cannot fly. It pauses, fluttering. It charges again at one of the panes, as if this time its speed is bound to break through the web in which it has been caught. Instead it hits the glass and is stunned. After each attack its bird-shaped box of little feathers is severely shaken and the heart inside beats faster than the wings. Under its beak hangs a little drop of blood. Each time it hits the glass there is another drop. Then, during the next, last, frantic circling, a miracle. It mistakes the window it is aiming itself at and flies through the one which is open. The bird knows immediately—before its tail has crossed the windowframe— that it is back in the sky. And it gives a chirp. A brief, barely audible but distinct chirp of joy.

Vica has arranged her skirt and is walking back home. At first I didn't believe in their names. Vico, Vica, it was too close to be true. It was a joke. But now Vica means this mistress whom I love and Vico means my master. This is our door.

Vico calls it the Hut. And Vica once called it the Pizza Hut. When she did so, there were tears in her eyes. In the outside corners of her eyes. I remember I had the impression that she had stopped herself crying so that no tears ran down her nose to her lips. With a great effort she had stopped herself crying, but about the little tears in the outside corners she could do nothing. She called it Pizza Hut to show how far it was from anything she had ever dreamt of living in! She had been born on the Prinsengracht, Amsterdam. Later I heard her call it "our pizzeria!" with a slightly drunken laugh. Vica drinks beer.

The Hut measures three metres by four. Before we built it Vica spent a whole day removing every stone from the twelve square metres of earth. Then she wet the soil and stamped on it and beat it at the edges with her swollen hands so as to make it as smooth as a table.

We built the walls with iron bed frames embedded side by side in the ground. Against them we fixed panels of polystyrene and scraps of plywood. Joachim offered us a pot of orange paint. He said it was too bright for him on his own. It was the colour for a family! he said.

She painted the panels orange and in places she left the white polystyrene untouched to give the effect of white stars. When Vico turns off the torch at night, they shine in the dark and we stare at them before we sleep.

One of the things the three of us agree about is sleep. I'm not sure which of us sleeps more lightly. Maybe we sleep deeply in turns. Sometimes I sleep on his side, sometimes on hers. I always sleep with them and I never sleep between them.

When we are asleep, the three of us together, we are protected. Nobody mucks around with us—like they did with the old man by the Central Station.

What we agree about is that sleep is best. Neither Vica nor Vico says this. Yet they know it's true. For nearly five years it's been true. Sleep is best. Our agreement that sleep is best, and the fact that we are three, lets our bodies relax after we've lain down.

When it's freezing and there's nothing to burn, which is often the case, they go to bed fully dressed and wearing gloves. Before they go to sleep each takes off a glove to hold the other's hand for a moment. Whilst they hold hands they stare at the cardboard ceiling, with

ART. NO. 353455B
c/ NO. 1 - 700
INHOUD 2 STUKS

printed on it. Then they turn over, knowing there's nothing better than sleep.

Vico and Vica. It's a joke they play. Changing their names to make a joke is a way of making a joke about the absurdity of things. No, let me correct myself—I often have to. Making a joke about their names is a way of laughing on the side about what has happened to them, and so, during two or three quick laughing breaths, forgetting the calamity.

The plastic sheet over our pieces of corrugated roofing is weighed down with broken chunks of concrete, but if there's a wind the rain finds its way through and the cardboard ceiling isn't waterproof and starts to drip and the large wet stains grow larger and larger.

Here the first hopelessness begins when you cannot imagine anything ever being dry again. The first hopelessness is damp.

Damp + cold = despair.
Despair + hunger = no god ever.
No god ever + alcohol = self-kill.

The wet season is over—this is what I want to tell Vica. It's going to be sunny. There'll be summer storms and we'll be soaked to the bone. But everything will dry quickly, this is what

I want to tell her. Wet will get dry without damp. The damp's over. This is what I want to tell her.

King, is it really sunny? she asks me. She is lying on the bed. If it's sunny, she says, we'll make two journeys and get four cans of water, okay? Vico will be pleased, King.

Fresh water is a problem for everyone in Saint Valéry and each one finds his own solution. Vica, however, uses more water than anybody else because she's always washing. There's always something on her clothesline. If you know where to look, you can see the washing on her line from the M.1000. On the right going north immediately after the overhead screen which tells you whether the traffic is jammed or fluid. To the left of the tyre dump.

This morning Vica and Vico argued for ten minutes about Vico's day. Chestnuts don't sell in the spring and it is too soon for us to get maize. So Vico wanted to take radishes. I can never believe, shouted Vica in the dark, never believe how stupid you are! People buy radishes from young girls! Perhaps from children. But never from an old man—an old man like you!

You'll make yourself a laughingstock! screeched Vica.

Of the two of them Vica is the better scavenger. Vico can't scavenge. He's still afraid his mother will see him.

To be a good scavenger you need to talk to what you're looking for and Vica knows this:

Come, little Cabbage, inside your brown leaves you're good!

There's still going to be a little white meat on you, Chicken, isn't there?

I want you, Saucepan. I don't care if you don't have a lid!

Let me sit on you, Chair. I'll find something to replace your missing fourth leg. Three legs are better than two!

Vica can do this; he can't.

Now Vica picks up a mustard glass from the floor by the bed and dips her fingers into it.

He says the mustard does no good and he's wrong, King, I know he's wrong. The mustard helps. They'd be rigid if I didn't do this every morning with the mustard. The swellings will never go and they look like hell. Three minutes each finger, half an hour for the two hands. I'm not sure which does the most good, whether it's each finger being rubbed or whether it's the exercise for the five fingers on the other hand doing the rubbing. Could it be both, my truffle? Can you imagine these hands when I was eighteen, playing Janacek? No, you can't.

> One day I met a Gypsy girl,
> lithe as a deer was she,
> black hair lay on her shoulders,
> her eyes were deep as the sea.

This is not the first time she has sung me this song. She sings it every other day and she has told me a hundred times about Janacek. Stories repeated over and over again become like pieces of furniture, and people have little furniture here so they repeat their stories. Vica does. Joachim does. Jack does . . .

The climb to get the water is cunning. The chariot which Vica stole from a supermarket is a cage on wheels. You could carry a man in it. We only fetch two twenty-litre jerry cans at a time because of the weight. The hard job is getting Vica up the bank with the cans. The bank is below the Elf garage. We leave the chariot at the bottom. She sits on my head, and I push her up with my neck and shoulders. Her feet, like her fingers, get swollen. We stop halfway up for her to catch her breath.

I lick her behind the knee as she sits on my head.

King! Fuck off! she says.

We fill the cans from the basins in the toilets behind the filling station. The man who runs the garage is at war with us.

You're stealing water! Get your fat arse out of here!

Today he doesn't dare approach us because I stand in the doorway facing him. He scowls.

I'm going to get a gun, he whispers.

Vica chews on her back teeth and pretends to ignore him.

After we've slid the full cans down the bank and loaded them, Vica slips a belt she has made for me over my chest and I haul the chariot back towards the Hut. And she follows, steering us like a plough.

It's no secret that I'm a little in love with Vica. She knows it. She knew it perfectly well when she was sewing together the pieces of the harness for the chariot. She makes use of my devotion.

Vico knows it too. Go and be with Vica! he says to me sometimes. He knows she prefers talking to me. She has already said everything to him many times. I'm new. I make people feel that whatever they tell, I'm hearing it for the first time. It's a gift I have: a kind of childish naivety. My eyes don't bear a trace of what they've seen.

So, with me, Vica relives her life in a way she can't do any more with Vico. At moments this makes him jealous. He comes back into the Hut, he sees me stretched out by the cooker which they use as a table, and Vica talking nonstop as she fingers a thing she has taken out of the bottle where they keep their treasures, and he lifts his arm and looking at me ferociously he shouts: Out! He shouts like a referee in a boxing match. And I go. It's better that way. I go out and piss.

I don't want to be in love with her. To survive I need to be single-minded, and I mean single. Vica, for her part, never decides, never sets out, to do something to attract me. Maybe it was different long ago. She and Vico met in Zurich in the '70s. He was negotiating a contract to supply working clothes for the city's municipal workers (if he is telling the truth about his factory) and she was studying for a term at the conservatory (if she really did study music). They met in a thunderstorm and he didn't take the train he intended back to Naples. She must have been seductive then. A question of concentration and footwork.

Today she's the least seductive woman imaginable. She does nothing to seduce. She behaves as if everybody around her was blind and deaf to her. She behaves, even when she is talking or looking at you, as if she were sitting on a bench alone. And this creates a problem. Because if you have fallen a little in love with her, you find you are in love with what she is, not what she does. I'm in love with what she is.

No, I have to correct myself again. It can happen that very briefly the old habit of using charm gets the better of her. Last spring we were selling daffodils by the post office near the Circus. There were twenty bunches in our red basin with a little water in it on the pavement. They were a crying-out yellow like the smell of leeks. We had picked them, hundreds of them, from the garden of a private house near the sea; the house was shuttered and bolted. Nobody ever comes there till the month of May. It was I who led them to the garden.

A schoolgirl bought two bunches and said, Thanks, Granny! And Vica, taken unawares, smiled and touched the cheek of the schoolgirl with her finger. At which the schoolgirl blew her a kiss and Vica lifted her stiff hand and blew two kisses back.

I haul and Vica steers the plough. By the time we get back home we are both panting and sweating.

I think I'll give you a bath! she says.

This is one of her regular jokes. When she's feeling good, she doesn't joke. She jokes when she's feeling bad.

In the winter we keep the water cans in the Hut, hoping they won't freeze. Last winter they froze solid, making the Hut even colder. When spring comes, like now, we keep them outside under a length of corrugated roofing, near the clothesline which runs from the roof of the Hut to the elder tree.

Let the rags dry in the sunshine! Vica screamed when we first moved in and Vico had fixed the line.

She calls everything "rags," even the new sheet we found in a laundry trolley outside the Park Hotel. Sometimes she washes something for one of the men living on the terrain. All right, I'll wash your rag if it's not too filthy, she offers.

We hump the cans to their place under the elder tree, and on top of the roofing she places the same red plastic basin we used for the daffodils.

In the tree she keeps a broom, suspended from the top branches. She takes it and begins to sweep the earth: first the earth floor of the Hut and then the path to where the red basin and the water cans live. Her sweeping is something I love about her. Nothing to do with any housewife crap or with keeping the home clean. She can't keep it clean. She wipes its nose every day, that's all. What I love is the way she moves her upper arms when she sweeps. Like a seal going down to the water over the rocks.

As if we haven't fucking well had enough today! she hisses and pokes the broom back up into the elder tree. Then she fetches two coffee cups from the Hut and washes them in the red basin. I watch her. She coughs and spits onto the broken earth.

Christ! she says.

She often suffers a moment of fatigue after steering the plough.

Remember what it used to be like? I say to comfort her. Nothing in your purse. No change coming ever. Only steps. Steps with the feet, little steps and your hands feeling in the sack. Steps with the cardigan that has no buttons. Words came out by themselves. Remember? Words like: Let the big pain not come yet! And no sooner were the words out than you changed your mind, clenched your teeth, and said: Let it! Let it! It's going to come soon, King, the big pain! The sooner the better!

This is what I want to tell her: The big pain didn't come. Not yet.

Let's eat a bit, King.

The door of the Hut opens outwards. It has three frosted-glass windows. Jack sold us the door. On the door frame on the inside, Vico screwed in three hooks for their tin mugs. Space is scarce.

If I go through the doorway and it's a freezing winter night, and they've found some wood to burn, I risk scorching my backside straightaway against the round iron stove. When it's hot the iron smells of beetroots.

We found the stove on a dump and brought it to Saint Valéry in the chariot. It took a long time to cover the six kilometres and I'll remember its name wherever I go. The letters were embossed between two embossed roses: GODIN.

Immediately after the stove there's a flat cooker also made of cast iron. This they use as a table, and in its oven they keep food. They never cook on it.

KING

On the cooker stands a glass jar, one of those jars in which women bottle fruit or vegetables, with a hinged lid and a red rubber washer to keep it airtight. They don't keep it shut and she uses it for keeping their private treasures in. It's a two-litre jar. The largest object is a Hohner mouth organ called The Big River Harp. As far as I can make out, neither of them ever played it. It is a treasure because they found it many years ago in a summer field where they fucked. They found it as they were getting to their feet. The other things in the jar I'll tell you about later. Behind it a calendar leans against the orange wall. Vico turns the page every month and each month shows a different kind of carpet in colour. For January a Tabriz carpet which was woven for Shah Thamasp the First, and underneath is written: "This is not a carpet but a white rose . . ." For February a Kerman carpet. And a carpet from Konya for April, the month we are in. Underneath this one is written: "When Marco Polo visited Konya in 1271 he said: Here are made the most beautiful carpets in the world with the most beautiful colours."

It's a calendar for last year, and, exceptionally, it was something Vico scavenged. After he brought it home, he spent two hours, the same evening, changing all the days of the week so they were up-to-date. On the orange wall above the calendar is where Vica's white stars shine.

Between the table and the bed there's very little space—just enough for your knees and feet if you are sitting on the edge of the bed, as Vica is now. She is sobbing. If I pay no attention to her, she'll stop.

The bed takes up a quarter of the ground space of the Hut and is in the corner opposite the door. The window, which Jack threw in with the door for the same price, because, he said, it was not right to see a couple of their age come to this, runs along the wall above the bed. It's a window which doesn't open, and it faces southeast, towards the sea. The sea is never visible but the fishy clouds above it are.

In the corner by the foot of the bed is what they call the kitchen: two gas burners on the top of a commode with a gas cylinder underneath. Between the commode and the foot of the bed there is just enough space for Vica to stand. Still sobbing, she's toasting some stale bread on one of the burners.

To the right of the commode stands a small wardrobe. When its door is open, it blocks the passageway to the outside door.

The wardrobe has three shelves. On these are arranged their clothes, tins and packets of food, a hairbrush, a toothbrush, spoons, plates, bottle opener, salt. Vica is looking for some margarine to put on her toast. She finds the packet behind an empty dog meat tin into which, last month, she planted a hyacinth bulb.

The plant has pushed itself out of the bulb, and the hyacinth flower, still green, has the shape and touch of a snake's head, a python's head. Next week, it will turn blue and its perfume will fill the Hut.

I refuse the toast Vica offers me.

We'd better go, King, and fetch the last two cans.

We get up to the Elf garage the same as we did before. Only this time the toilet door is locked. Vica tries the handle with both hands.

The fucking mean bastard! she swears and starts to go back down the slope, sticking the heels of her boots into the smashed rubble for which there is no word.

Wait! I tell her. There's somebody in the toilet.

She looks at me furiously and sits down. We wait for ten minutes, neither of us opening our mouths. I nudge her and the door opens and a young woman comes out holding a key and a hair-dryer whose cord is trailing on the ground. Her hair is shiny and damp.

Vica goes regally towards her. She has the capacity, Vica, of making a stranger not see the stains on her skirt and the dust on her boots, and this is due to the way she moves forward, bosom first. It's not confidence—her confidence was smashed long ago; she plants her feet like she does because her legs were made like that and they can't do otherwise.

The young woman, tossing her head so that her hair flicks back, extends her hand and says, He gave me the key and told me to lock it when I'd finished. But I'll give it to you and you can give it back to him when you're finished, okay?

I have spotted what I take to be her car: an Opel.

I'll see he gets it back, says Vica.

What's his name? asks the young woman. On her right hand she's wearing, I notice, a gold ring with a large blue stone. Probably a lapis lazuli.

His name?

He has such intelligent eyes!

Somebody has to be intelligent.

Doesn't he fret in the car?

Never, says Vica, I wind the window down a little and he likes the air, he likes the feel of it rushing past. He never frets.

Far to go?

Vica looks at me with her ageless eyes. Amsterdam, she says.

That's a long way, says the young woman.

We'll be there tomorrow if we drive all night, says Vica.

Bonne route! says the young woman with the blue jewel in her ring and she trips away, her hands resting on the air as if it was a balustrade.

Quick now! I tell Vica and I nip her bottom.

According to Vico, the Babylonians believed there were male and female lapis lazuli. The ones with more light in them were female.

We slide the two filled cans down the slope. Vica gets them into the chariot. I pull and she follows, steering the plough.

When we reach home, the first thing she does is to take the key of the garage toilet out of her coat pocket and drop it into the bottle with the other treasures. Then she changes into her outsize jeans. She wears a skirt only in Saint Valéry. In town she wears blue jeans, as many sweaters as she needs, and a black anorak she found in the park.

A figure fills the open doorway and blocks the light. I heard him coming and knew his measured step. It's Jack the Baron, as Vico calls him. He's big. It is a long time since he had his hair cut. He has the eyes of a Great Dane.

Nine months ago, when Vico and I first came to Saint Valéry, Jack wasn't going to take us. I don't know how Vico heard about the place. He told Vica later that he'd heard about it from a dying man, that it was a kind of heritage. Anyway, when we got here, Jack took a look at us and said:

No question, we're full, no sites left.

I'm ready to pay, Vico said.

It's not a question of payment, kid, it's a question of choice.

May I ask you how you choose?

By what I see, and you look like a loose nut. I'll take the dog but not you. Scram!

I'm afraid I have to wait for my wife, she's coming to meet us here, Vico said.

You have a wife? I thought you only had a dog.

Yes, I have a wife.

Why the hell didn't you say so before, man? Is she infirm?

No.

If you have a wife, I'll take you.

We have been married thirty years.

You know how much the down payment is, man?

I was told one thousand five hundred.

Who told you that?

An acquaintance called Hans who died.

Since his time it's gone up. Today it's two thousand five hundred. Have you got it? You don't look like it.

Give me two days and I'll pay you, said Vico. And when I pay you, we build where?

Here.

Here?

Here by this elder tree. I've a door and a window I'll throw in for the same price. I thought you just had a dog, I didn't know you had a wife, a wife makes a big difference.

Vico paid Jack the two thousand five hundred Jack was asking for by selling a camera. He had kept this camera in a sack with woolen socks wrapped round it. Like this it was hidden and didn't get stolen on the street and like this it didn't get scratched. I went with him to sell it. It was the end of the autumn.

Vico looked like a man who when it is snowing shambles into the public library to keep warm. He is illiterate and he has scavenged a pair of glasses to suggest that he is a regular reader, and the librarians leave him alone in the warmth whilst he watches the girls from the lycée consulting their encyclopedias. Vico was not this man. He had read thousands of books in his life, but he had come to look like this man.

We enter the shop. His spectacles are on his nose.

How much are you prepared to offer me for this Canon 42? he asks.

Bayonet or screw?

Screw.

That means it's old. Let me see it.

In perfect condition, says Vico, handing it over, with a 35–80 zoom.

Have you a bill or guarantee?

For Christ's sake, says Vico.

At this point the shopkeeper suspects the camera has been stolen. He glances at me and his suspicion becomes a certainty.

Where did you buy it?

In Rome.

In Rome? Rome is a very long way away. This model has been superseded and I would have considerable difficulty in selling it. I'm afraid we are not interested.

Yes, I bought it in Rome.

Yet you have no papers?

None. It has a double flash mechanism so you don't get red eyes in your portraits.

You don't get red eyes anyway!

The shopkeeper is beginning to hate us. He wants to say to Vico: You have red eyes and there's no flash and there never will be, get out of my shop! He is preparing to say this.

Do you want to know the photos I've taken with the camera you are holding in your hands? asks Vico in his butterfly voice.

We are not interested, says the shop man.

The camera in your hands has taken photos of the pyramids of Giza in Egypt, of the Stadium in Aphrodisias, of the Roman garrison town of Timgad in Algeria with its Roman theatre which has three thousand five hundred places, of the Certosa di San Martino in Napoli, of the Tower of Chimarron on Naxos, of the Temple of Hera in Paestum.

You have travelled a lot, but we are not interested. It has been superseded.

It's in perfect condition and its timing is still perfect, down to a fifteen-hundredth of a second.

Our clients today prefer automatic cameras.

With this Canon 42 I intended to take pictures in the north of Europe, the Central Station of Helsinki for example, the Rietveld Schröder house in Utrecht, the garden suburb in Darmstadt which was financed by the Archduke of Hesse. Today a Canon 42 is worth ten thousand, and because we are in a hurry I'll let you have it for five.

Why are you in such a hurry? asks the shopkeeper.

Because it's spring, mutters Vico.

The shopkeeper hangs the camera on his shoulder, opens the till drawer, and takes out three notes of a thousand and puts them on the counter.

This is the maximum, he says, take it or leave it.

Vico picks up the money.

I had no choice, he told me when we were outside in the street.

Now I understand why Jack the Baron said at the beginning that having a wife made a big difference. Few couples survive the calamity as a couple. The sight of the other makes things worse for each of them. A couple is a rarity, above all an elderly couple. In Jack's soldier's mind an elderly couple were a little like royalty.

This morning Jack has shaved and smoothed down his hair with water.

I have to go into the city centre, he says. Will you stay for once? We can't leave the place alone. It's too dangerous.

I don't like to disappoint, she says, but I have to meet Vico.

Then leave King to guard us.

King will stay, she says.

When Vica is pleased, not only her mouth but her neck smiles. And for an instant she's pleased at the idea of outwitting Jack. I can see it in her neck, and this pleasure spreads out into a kind of benevolence.

I love your jacket, she tells him.

Jack pretends not to have heard her; he prefers his jackets to be noticed and not commented upon.

I have a meeting at ten, he says, so if you're going to pay me a coffee, be quick about it.

No milk, she says.

Unnecessary, he says.

Jack as I told you makes his jackets himself. He makes them from paper, cut and sewn together as if it was cloth. The one he is wearing this morning has been made from the pages of a flower-seed catalog. He calls it his phlox jacket. He has another one made from maps. They are well cut and they have brass buttons like blazers.

I have to go to the City Hall, he says, I've been hearing things I don't like the sound of.

Vica opens the cupboard to see if there's sugar. Jack waits in the doorway, the phlox flowers of his jacket violet white and pink in the light filtering through the window.

I don't take sugar.

Nor do we, she says, although it's not true—she says it because there isn't any.

I'm going to find out and I'm going to warn them, Jack says. He has the neck of a ram.

At the City Hall? she asks.

It sounds as if it's none too soon, he says. Then he smiles an old soldier's smile, intended to reassure Vica and to remind her of the dangers he is going to save her from.

She ties a scarf over her head. She never goes downtown without a scarf. She has two: one gold-coloured and the other black. I prefer it when she wears the black one, it's safer.

King will stay, she says.

Through the doorway I watch the two of them make their way towards Ardeatina Street. Because of his jacket it looks as though she's walking across the wasteland with a flowering bush. Whenever Jack puts on one of his handmade jackets—he has four and he wears them only on Sundays or when he goes downtown—he looks at himself sideways in the mirror in his shack and whispers:

Once upon a time I knew a good woman.
Once upon a woman I had a good time.

This joke invariably makes him straighten his back and take on the bearing of the sergeant he once was.

I see Vica stumble over something and Jack puts a large hand under her elbow to steady her. Then she takes his arm and I watch them walking like a couple until they disappear.

Saint Valéry is now mine alone to guard. I go outside and I scramble to the top of the scrap mountain. From here I can survey the whole coat. Our Hut, Jack's house, Corinna's van, Danny's container, Anna's blockhouse, Joachim's tent, Saul's Rancho, Alfonso's place, Liberto's place.

While I'm doing nothing at all, I spot two men coming across from Ardeatina Street. Strangers. No one strolls here. It's no Ramblas. Nobody comes here for nothing. I face a choice. I'm faster, much faster, than they. Do I outflank them and hassle them from behind, the chaser is usually at an advantage? Or do I get back on the path and go to meet them? They are big, young, and they don't look innocent. Any general would happily enlist them as soldiers for his mercenary army. I choose the path, where the coat would button up.

KING

My advantage is that they're two. They've seen me. If only I can keep it frontal. If they separate, I'm lost. One of them has started picking up stones. I walk slowly, poised between each step, as if testing the path before putting my weight on it. He throws the first stone. It misses.

As soon as they are more than one, men get distracted. This is my hope. I'm close enough now to make them both remember the possibility of flight. They have stopped walking. The man throws a second stone clumsily which grazes my head. They hear me growling and watch my eyes.

Gimme one of your stones, the second man says, I'll get the dog! And they glance at each other, as I hoped, during a fraction of a second.

A fraction of a second is long enough for the dog's advantage of surprise. It is as long as the moment when the bird knew—before its tail had crossed the windowframe—that it was back in the sky. In that fraction, whilst their eyes are turned away, I leap at the man with the stones, all my weight flung against his chest. He falls onto his back.

At this point I'm clever. I stand off to give him time to leave, and both men run from the path in opposite directions. The general has called off the invasion. If I hadn't stood off, they'd have eventually killed me. A dog's timing takes learning.

I trot round the coat and visit the Boeing. Then I end up in the spot where Marcello likes to sunbathe. Here I lie down and shut my eyes. I'm not asleep. I can hear any arrival. I see a beach. Nobody goes to it except me. My beach is four kilometres southeast of Saint Valéry, across the river which flows into the sea there. Over the river are three bridges, each one with a Roman arch. They are not used by traffic any longer. Two are more or less broken down, and the third has grass growing on it. I don't know why they were built so close together. The river there is like a finger wearing three rings. Terns and cormorants and skuas fly low over the water. What I like is that when I'm at the top of the arch, trotting on the grass, which has covered the stones of the bridge, everything runs downhill away from me, as far as the waves. Isn't pleasure itself often a sweet incline like that? Nearly every pleasure?

The sea has drawn back farther than usual and I reach the edge of the kelp forest. The kelp is as green as fern and underneath it is dark, a damp dark, smelling of pale skin and shining teeth. My nose begins to twitch. Everywhere the wet vivid colours of organs inside a body.

A scallop under the tangle has just shut up his shell. I heard the click. Under a rock there's some yellow coral in the shape of a cow's teats and instead of milk shooting out of them, a cobweb of grey drops dripping. I part the eelgrass, it touches my ears. There's nothing on shore as green and sinuous as eelgrass and it smells of birth.

On the other side of the eelgrass I find my friend, the hermit crab. Call me Torgny, he told me. I find him at home. I call him Tor. He lives in a whelk shell. He sits in his home, for his hind-quarters have no carapace and are therefore unprotected. Without his whelk he wouldn't last an hour. When some bastard tries to muck around with him he retracts completely into his whelk and blocks the entrance with his right pincer. His right pincer is larger than his left so he can use it like a front door. He lives with several anemones who have loose hair, blue and golden. They are attached to the outside of the whelk.

What's new? he asks.

Nothing, I say.

Living together suits them. The anemones can't get around by themselves, and with Torgny they have transport. Walking on his powerful, bent front legs, he shifts the shell around and like this the anemones get more to eat. They eat out every night. In exchange they protect him, since their flowing locks contain a poison which discourages attacks—particularly by octopi.

Troubles never come singly, says Tor. I've got to move. Carapace too small. I've found a new whelk which is a good bit bigger. As soon as I move in, I'll get rid of the carapace. Unbelievably tight across the chest. The problem, as always, is the anemones. They don't want to leave the old shelter. Talk to them, King, if you can.

Sweetie, I say to the youngest, you come first and you'll get the best place on the new shell.

She flicks her head and ignores me.

He's the owner! I growl. Do you hear me? He's the owner and he's turning you out, all of you! Get moving.

They let their golden and blue locks trail and they play deaf.

Let us pray together in the darkness, Torgny says to them, let us pray together in our affliction and I will carry you all on my back to our new home, and our salvation.

The bitches tighten their suction disks and cling to the old whelk more fiercely than ever.

I go right up close to them and I ask very quietly: Do you want to die, one by one, and alone? Well, do you?

This works. One by one they go still. They retract their tentacles and they roll themselves up like rosebuds. Then they let the hermit crab carry them on his back, one after the other, to their new place where they will live for a while, until one day they will have to move again.

Look, King! says Tor before he joins them, look!

He braces his massive shoulders, he has shoulders like Jack, and the carapace cracks and falls in pieces onto the seabed. On its inside it is chalky white, and its outside is vixen coloured.

Get in quick, Tor, I say to him.

And at the same moment I hear another cascade of something like small stones and I open one eye. Jack is coming back round the Sink. I get to my feet and, although he is far away, I can see his jacket is torn. A bad sign.

1:30 P.M.

I skirt the Sink, which is a pond of stagnant water. A few days ago I found a frog there, defiant, blown up with courage, and he jumped with a single leap at the very last moment back into the water. He was more white than green, for frogs turn whitish during the winter.

I cross the terrain, clamber up a bank of rubble, and start to run. The sun in the sky is like a stone which Vico has thrown for his dog to fetch. I have a strange way of talking, for I'm not sure who I am. Many things conspire to take a name away. The name dies and even the pain suffered doesn't belong to it any more. I'm making for the Circus in the city centre.

In the sunshine I swerve for the hell of it, and I prance when I cross the road. People used to get alarmed when they saw a dog running alone in the street. It reminded them of theft. Today the little alarm created by a running dog is more reassuring than the screeching alarms of parked cars and shop windows and wired residences even when nobody is tampering with them. Today everything is disappearing, yet there's no thief visible since the thieves are offshore. This has made the dog's little alarm almost welcome. The people along Ardeatina Street look at me, eyebrows raised, noses wrinkled, and their open mouths almost smiling.

An old man has brought a folding camp chair with him so he can sit down when he is tired after walking a few hundred metres.

Many walls in the city are sprayed with dog paintings. I run past a rhinoceros in a green suit, Liberty without her cloak on, eight letters making NICE TIME. When it's sprayed everything is a love name. A pair of lips as red and large as a cow's liver. Four letters coupling to make RISK.

The diesel lorries pass. A mother with a child on her back changes arms to carry the shopping bag in the hand which is less tired.

Three kids on skates race past. I change course to join them and put myself in the middle. Two girls and a boy.

Let it last forever! their look says, and they dance to this look, very slowly, held by their speed, like gulls are held by the wind above a ship. I watch their legs. I keep up with their legs and their ankles which bend and their knees which drive.

The boy's legs are not like the girls'! A man's legs are for landing, they are made to absorb the shock of arrival. We have arrived together, a man's legs say, the two of us.

The girls' legs are for leaving. Forever leaving. We are on the point of going and now you have arrived, so where shall we go?

Human beings were made for dancing. They were. Only when they're dancing does all they can do, all their capacities and ingenuity, all their tricks and deceits, and all their terrible truthfulness become gift, pure gift. Tango beings.

A bus hoots, the driver swearing and prodding his fingers, and we jump back to where we can circle, and there are pigeons. I race around the dancers on their skates and the pigeons fly into the air.

Hey, boy! one of the girls shouts, leg in the air and the other leg bent as she glides forward, you're hungry, aren't you?

He's a thin dog!

What's your name, tell us your name!

He's got a collar at least.

Can you read it?

Careful. Don't scare him, he may be vicious.

Where do you think he belongs?

Perhaps he'd like the rest of my Big Mac. Hey, boy!

She takes the carton out of her knapsack, opens the lid, and places half a Big Mac on the ground for me. When she bends down, her ankle quivers because her heel lifts the skate off the pavement. I wolf the Mac and make off.

None of them is laughing any longer. Their arms hang limp and their hands are not touching. Their sense of destiny has gone.

I stop running. I walk, head up, back straight, to indicate that I know exactly where I am heading and that I am awaited there. Otherwise, in this district I risk being picked up as a stray.

Two women who haven't seen one another for a long while have met by chance on the corner. They are even older than Vica. They want to embrace, I can see, but their backs are too stiff, they cannot easily bend forward. So they bend their knees, both of them, until their knees touch and hold them up. Then, with their necks out, they kiss each other on the cheek.

Vica, whenever she's on her way to the Circus, stops, if she has time, at the Church of Santa Maria. Vico never goes to church. It is a small difference which offers them something to talk about. There is little to talk about when there is no future, and subjects are welcome.

You went to the Santa Maria? asks Vico.

Naturally, says Vica.

And you prayed?

Of course. I prayed for you, I prayed for King, I prayed for myself, I prayed for us all. And it's quiet in there. You could take a nap.

Prayers make as much din as pigeons! says Vico.

It's warm too, says Vica.

They were at the Circus, installed beside the delivery door of a cut-price shoe shop. It was winter, and they were selling chestnuts. Vico had converted a TOTAL oil drum into a brazier, which they carried in the chariot.

Chestnuts being roasted smell of scorched wood and good meat. Even the early morning drunk can smell their aroma from the other side of the road, and so you don't have to shout to attract buyers. Vico would starve rather than shout. With chestnuts the appetizing smell does the work for him. When Vica is there, she shouts.

To turn the chestnuts over so they don't get charred, Vica uses an old teaspoon which she keeps in her jacket pocket. Vico uses his fingers. As a result, his fingers are calloused and feel as scaly as shrimps, though not fishy. They are warm and dry, their skin like the paper you put at the bottom of a cake tin.

Stations, libraries, trains, staircases, yes, I'll sleep in them, Vica, but I'm not going to sleep in a church!

I don't sleep there either.

You were saying I might, and I say no.

They are done now, says Vica about the chestnuts, you can put them in the paper.

The chestnuts before being roasted have to be cut, otherwise they explode. One nick of a knife down their length from head to foot. Then over the heat, and thanks to the slit, their hides open like unbuttoned coats. And their hot flesh, a little powdery in places and wrinkled in others, is exposed and cries out to be eaten.

Walking prudently along the sidewalk, avoiding the gutter on one side and the building entrances with their surveillance video cameras on the other, I look across the street at Vica's Church of Santa Maria. Its columns are like the fingers of a hand on which the tower is resting its chin. Behind the ears and the head, white clouds are being blown from the west. The expression of the tower is one of amazement. Its mouth is wide open. Watching the Church of Santa Maria, I don't notice where I am walking. I realize it too late.

What a shite you are! growls the dog.

And you, Rottweiler, you who work for the pigs! I reply, for I see the mess I'm in.

You got one bitten ear, you want another? he threatens.

Watch it now, you grey dog, dog who works for the pigs for a dog's pittance, watch the glove come off the teeth! Watch it, dog!

He is on a short leash and he can't touch me. He is, all the same, his master's intelligence. His master is wearing a belt and holster and has thick fingers. At this moment his master is eyeing a babe as she gets out of a taxi which has drawn up to the entrance of a hotel where there are three men in cherry uniforms arranging suitcases. I must not let a single hair retract, for Rottweiler will spot it. I have to impress him immediately, so much that he relays no message at all to his master. Otherwise it's the Pound. I need to show him I'm fearless because I have backing, because I have countless connections, inestimable prestige. Where does the courage come from? From the ground, up through the paws.

Watch the glove come off the teeth, I say, watch it now! I'm unquestionable!

Rottweiler is getting lazy, so he is convinced. His forehead smooths out and his two eyes fold into slits, whilst his master gapes at how the babe's arse moves. I walk on, heart tapping my ribs.

To slit the chestnuts you need a good knife, sturdy, sharp, and not too big. Chestnut in the left hand between finger and thumb and one incision with the point of the knife clasped in the right hand.

Do you know what wealth is when you're a kid? Vico asked me one day when he was in a good mood. When you're a kid, wealth is a knife in one trouser pocket and an electric torch in the other.

No, said Vica, when you're a kid wealth is a little red leather book with telephone numbers in it.

KING

A few days later, lying beside the chestnut brazier, something came to me between the ears: the world is so bad, God has to exist. I asked Vico what he thought.

Most people, he said quickly, would draw the opposite conclusion.

As he said this he dropped several hot chestnuts into one of the packets which Vica staples together from old colour magazines.

I'm thinking of the forest, I told him.

You talk every day about the forest, he said.

No, it depends on the season.

Homesickness. Mal du pays. Nostalgia, he said.

You can't see sunlight in the forest and not admit it's beautiful, I said, looking straight at Vica, who was sitting on the pavement with her back against the delivery door. The world is well made, every leaf of it. Only men are vile.

That's right, she said, only men.

Some of the vilest have been women, Vico said.

Women are beautiful as birch trees, I said.

King, you don't know what you're talking about!

I'm talking about God. The second packet of chestnuts was full now and Vico was waving his fingers in the air to cool them. I'm talking about God. If the world of men is vile and the rest so well made, there has to be a force for evil. Nothing else makes sense.

Ignorance and stupidity, said Vico, nicking with the knife a new lot of chestnuts before arranging them on the brazier.

It's not the ignorant who do evil, said Vica, it's the clever ones.

If there's a force for evil, there has to be a force for good. No? And that means God, I said.

For Christ's sake, throw him a chestnut!

If everything was as beautiful as the forest, I'd never believe in him, I told them. It's the shit which makes me believe.

Neither of them answered. After a while there's no more to say.

The handle of Vico's knife is made of ram's horn. When shut, it's a little longer than his hand is wide. To open, you pull out and flick. To shut, you press on the spine opposite the blade. The silhouette of the steel blade is like a woman dancing the tango.

I take a shortcut through some backstreets, they're safer for me on my own. I look as though I belong here. These streets, though, are dangerous for sleeping. At night the people who live here come home and believe that the street is their own corridor, where they can do exactly what they need and want, immediately. These narrow streets are like the final night—there's no time to lose in them. The tarts do a brisk trade in their little rooms, and the pimps carry guns. Now in the still afternoon heat the only sound is that of a tennis ball.

A boy is throwing it against a blind wall in a square where there's a cheap fish restaurant. It's shut now. The boy has been doing this for what seems to him a long time. There are no surprises left; he has learnt by heart the wall and the ball, and both of them are as listless as he is.

To make a little change—it is much more difficult to change anything than you talkers believe—he decides to catch the ball as it comes back, at the very last moment, before it bounces on the paving stones between the stains and the scraps of paper and the dog shit and the fish bones. He watches the ball coming, he waits, he savors the moment of doing nothing when he's at one with the overwhelming force which makes it so difficult to change anything, and he stoops forward to catch the ball a hand's breadth from the ground. The next time, the ball comes a little harder, and after the sweetly drawn-out wait all he has to do is to bend his knees and catch it between his heels.

The third time, he misjudges and the ball hits the ground. He does nothing, he waits as before, but far longer. He stares at the wall, the wall stares at the ball, which rolled and was stopped by an empty beer can. The ball stares at the boy, the boy scratches his tummy and goes on waiting. Three cats are stretched out, hungry and asleep, by the fish restaurant.

Eventually the boy goes dutifully to pick up the ball and returns to his old position before the wall. He will start again. What else?

At this moment I make him see me. His eyes open a little wider. Hey! he says.

I open my mouth.

Do you want to play?

He bounces the ball on the ground and I jump at it and don't catch it. Why should I?

Let's play, he says. We play like this. I throw it against the wall and when the wall sends it back you have to catch it before I do. If you don't, I've won!

And if I catch it?

If you catch it first, we do something more difficult, okay?

Like what?

He smiles for the first time.

He throws the ball and I don't follow. He throws it again so it comes back from the wall in my direction and I catch it easily.

So let's go, I tell him.

This time he hurls the ball into the angle where the wall joins another wall and the ball ricochets. I haven't seen this before and he has, so he's in the right place and I'm not. Like I say, it's more difficult to change anything than talkers believe.

KING

He repeats the trick and this time I'm there and we jump and hit each other in midair, missing the ball, both of us. He falls on top of me and there we are, both laughing on the ground.

I get to my feet and go and fetch the ball.

Give! he shouts.

I run away with it and he chases me. Abruptly I turn round to face him and drop the ball, mouth open.

I think a game will start. We are four, and with four a game is possible. The boy, the ball, the wall, and myself.

The four of us against the afternoon.

The boy throws hard and high up. If the blind wall had windows, it would be as high as the second storey. Lower down there is dog art. Letters, taller than the boy, hunch themselves up, like Torgny's anemones, into gigantic rosebuds, red and white. Only a dog can read them easily. These dog letters say: DON'T RUN AWAY.

The ball nicks the angle of the wall, who sends it back fast and spinning to my right, as I foresaw he would, so I'm there. I catch it volleying, I pause to get my balance, and I toss it softly to the ground at the boy's feet.

Let's go, the four of us say together.

The boy flings the ball again and I catch it. Then again and again.

Each time it is different, each time the ball, the angle of the wall, he, and I play a different game which is still the same game, and each time all four of us get faster, the last one telling the next one where to go.

The speed takes us in its huge hand and holds us up like the sea does when you are swimming, so that soon we are floating out of our depth, our feet no longer touching the ground.

It goes faster and faster, the ball twinkling, the boy screaming, the angle of the wall winking in the sunlight, and me snapping till nothing else exists. When we do change something, it changes quicker than you talkers believe. The cats have fled. The speed bends us all.

Some other dog letters at the very bottom of the wall spell: END OF THE WORLD. The boy throws the ball too low and it hits the W of the WORLD. The angle of the wall can't gather it and I can't get there.

Sooner or later it had to break since we were breathless, we had no more breath. The ball rolls to the other side of the square to sleep. The angle of the wall dissolves in the sunshine. The boy and I bury our laughing mouths in each other's shoulders, our ears touching.

The boy gets his breath back.

What a day! he says, his eyes wide open and a little snot from his nose making his smiling mouth glisten. I lick him.

His words are exactly the same as those which Jack used on his return to Saint Valéry this morning.

KING

What a day! Jack said.

His jacket was torn as if somebody had picked him up by the back of the collar to throw him out, and his left sleeve was ripped from elbow to cuff, as if he had turned round to punch the man who tried to throw him out. I didn't ask him what had happened.

He must have hurried back, because he was sweating profusely and the salt of his sweat was making his eyes water.

You're off, King? he asked me.

I nodded. He scowled and retracted his head a little into his shoulders. Listen, he said, if you see any of them in town—any except Corinna—tell them to come back quick. As quick as they can.

Something bad happened?

You ask too many questions.

It's my nature!

It's not a day for joking, King.

He lifted his head and looked over Ardeatina towards the city. One thing hiding another. The office tower blocks touching the sky. The sky lying on top of the invisible sea. A window flashing. A crane turning. The howl in our ears. He seemed to be searching for something. There are men who gain time like this, and during the time gained they grow stronger, they recover

the strength which comes from a reminder of their habitual solitude and endurance. Such men have slow reactions and you can
trust them.

I gave them something to think about, he said, but it's not
over, by no means over. If you see any of them, bring them back,
there's a good dog.

Jack walked solemnly towards his place.

The boy in the square wants to come with me and I tell him
no, he should stay here. I ask him where he lives.

Nobody gets as fast as we did! he shouts.

So I leave him and slip through a passageway to the Aventin
district, where there is a building with balconies, four storeys
high, and holding up the balconies there are carved women
without clothes.

They were the sign, Vico said, of a confident civilization
which displayed in public art what it liked to enjoy in secret.

You could do guided tours! snapped Vica.

The carved woman on the corner of the top floor, whose
breasts are lime white with bird shit, is pointing with her right
hand to a concrete wall. Follow where she's pointing. The dog
letters say: THE MAD AND THE INSANE. Turn right and
find an alley where there's a pinched hand in blue. The alley
comes out by a metal staircase climbing up to an overhead rail-
way station.

Beneath this staircase most mornings there's Achilles. He's usually cut up because he provokes fights and they smash bottles on him. He's a brutal victim. There are many here. Brutal winners are much harder to recognise, for their brutality is hidden by their winnings. The brutality of the defeated stares at you. Most mornings there's blood on his face.

When he lies down under the metal staircase to sleep, his bitch takes up a curious position. Her hindquarters stay on the pavement. And all the rest of her lies sprawling on top of Achilles the warrior. Every night. Like this her weight puts its arms round the poor fucker so he can remember only one thing and forget the rest.

> Want a date
>   with a foothold
> Hanging from hands
>   wrists half broken
> Years since clean nails
>   or clean collar
> Don't slip now
>   slip knot
> A little kick
>   so as to be quick
> gone

I cross Treptower Park. On my left runs the ancient city wall of red bricks which smell of graves. The dead are under the earth everywhere here. The first leaves on the trees are hanging out, millions of them, curly and pale like the sounds kids make before they've learnt to speak words. A magnolia tree is in flower, and onto the grass around it petals have fallen. Like the cups of tiny brassieres.

Shut your mouth! hisses Vica.

I piss against the tree, and whilst I piss, I watch a man who is sitting on a bench speaking into his flip-phone. He has a jacket as well cut as Jack's but made of fine cotton with a lot of white thread in it. The white thread gives his jacket a chromium shine. His telephone is black.

I'm buying good-will, he says, it's a priority, and the returns are coming in, sure, no question . . .

One of Alfonso's loser's songs is about a magnolia. A song for the winter, explains Alfonso, when the metro's warm and the passengers' shoes are damp, the season when, if a man stays in the metro for seven days and nights without going up to the street, he'll never leave, he'll have to be carried out.

It's too late, says the man in the chromium jacket into the telephone, they've taken the offer! No, Duke, you can't do that. If you do that you make me a liar and you can't do that.

His eyes make very small glances, like the eyes of a man operating a video game.

Yes, that's why I am saying, you make me a liar. I'm not operating under these conditions.

The first daisies with violet fringes are opening out on the grass.

Listen, I'm warning you, he says, I'm warning you now, this Wednesday morning, if I don't get confirmation by tomorrow P.M., tomorrow, Thursday, if I don't get confirmation, I'm going across the street and you know as well as I do what I'll be taking with me!

His throat contracts and he is obliged to swallow so that his pink ears move.

I'm giving you till Thursday P.M. If I don't get confirmation from you by Thursday P.M., I'm going across the street, is that clear?

He closes the telephone and shoots his cuffs. Then he adjusts his collar. His chin is still thrust forward like a boy's; he doesn't know what happens when the bluffs are called. He'll remain a boy for as long as he wins.

He shakes his telephone as if it's got water in it and calls another number. Faster than you think, my sweet, he says, much faster, but I'll get there.

His voice tells me he is talking to a woman. Now he listens and, whilst listening, takes a calculator out of his pocket and starts touching the keys. He looks up.

Scram! he shouts and makes an empty gesture of throwing a stone at me. Scram!

I ignore him. The earth here in the park smells of abandonment, like a house which hasn't been lived in for fifty years.

Out of the corner of my eye I spotted, a while ago, a squirrel who wants to flirt. Where are you from, sailor? she'll ask. But the earth smells of abandonment, too many dead left here, left centuries ago without any intention of coming back, so their absence grows sharper and sharper. Each day it becomes more clear that they are not going to relent, they have gone for good.

The man with the chromium jacket gets another number. Book me a plane this evening to London, he says.

I approach and I frighten him. Which is what I intended to do. He knows all the rules of the game and he has everything set up. Yet my snaps are not in the game, and the boy in him is obsessed by my teeth. He can't take his eyes off them when I growl.

I'm watching his eyes. He makes as if to run for it along the path, so I snap at his heels. He jumps, standing up, onto a bench, eyes vacant. I settle on the path to keep him there. He stands on the bench, indecisive.

Good dog, he says, you're a good dog, aren't you?

I behave as if my ears, which are standing up, are deaf.

Where do you live? he asks sweetly. Have you got a home?

I growl.

We'll be friends, won't we?

He doesn't know I can talk, yet in this situation he'd like me to reply.

I do not make a sound.

You know, he says slowly as if talking to a child, I still have a lot to do today.

You're lucky! I suddenly reply.

He is so surprised, so taken aback, that he slips his flip-phone into his jacket pocket and stands there, hands hiding his crotch.

Christ! he whispers.

Out of the corner of my eye I see a squirrel approaching. I stare at the man for a moment longer and then, like the dead, I leave.

When I turn round, he is on the path, brushing down his trousers with his hand.

You're going to buy me breakfast? asks the squirrel, I haven't had any breakfast.

I take the outside staircase, which climbs to the top of the hill on which the Church of Saint Agostino is built and from which you can see the sea.

I'm going to propose a trip to Vico and Vica. I have a friend who's a fisherman. He's called Anders. He has blue eyes, he wears a woolen cap all the year round, and his face is the colour of a razor shell. It's not that he is a kind man; he's an expert in harshness. His boat is named the *Galena*, which is the name of a stone.

I've been out with him. I lie on the deck and watch the coast-line rock.

What are you looking so happy for? he says. You know nothing.

Dogs swimming in the sea look like porpoises, and porpoises were the friends of sailors. I have vague memories of another life with sailors. A sea-life which comes back to me sometimes after fucking. It was a life with more jokes in it than this one. Maybe not more laughter, but more jokes.

Vico says Porpoise can have nothing to do with Dog for the name Porpoise comes from the word Porc meaning Pig. Which is another example of how names can be wrong. More than half the things which exist have been misnamed—men aren't strong at naming.

On the deck of Anders' boat happiness comes, and this is what I'd like to explain to them—happiness comes because on the deck of the *Galena* you're no longer in the city, you're free of it. On land wherever you go and however far you go, you take the place with you. You can't get rid of it. On Anders' boat— only one kilometre out to sea—you're free of the city, its name doesn't choke you any more, and the boat rocks.

The cold out there, when it's cold, comes from the northwest wind and the spray whipped from the waves. It comes from nothing else.

The boat rides the waves and is going where Anders wants. At sea you can navigate. This is what I will tell Vico. On the deck of the *Galena*, I want to tell him, Vica will sing. And if the two of them don't want to come back, they don't have to. It's deep there.

3:00 P.M.

The radishes didn't sell. Vico is sitting in the delivery doorway of the shoe shop which has permanent sales and a permanent notice in the window which says: 50% OFF ON THE SEC-OND PAIR. His head is nodding. The pigeons on the ledge above nod quickly. To my surprise, Vica isn't here. If it was the other way round, I'd be worried. Vico could get seriously lost but not Vica. She is probably drinking a can of beer. She may be singing.

He has shut his eyes; I can tell he's not asleep; he wants to be. The radishes are in a cardboard box on the sidewalk by his left hand. To his right, with a chain around its wheels, is our second chariot. The chain makes it harder to nick. Radishes have the underground redness of beetroots except there's no white in beetroots. The fingers of Vico's hand resting on the sidewalk are twitching . Radish white has in it the flavour of aluminum.

I once knew a truffle bitch from the south. Her master, she claimed, was offered twenty thousand for her. And he preferred to keep me! She announced this with her tongue out. You should see us! she told me. We work all day in the month of September, when the days are still long, and we come home with five, six, seven kilos. I'm talking about the black ones. In May we go for the white ones. The white are more discreet and their flavour is younger.

Truffles, I ask her, what do they smell like? Sex, she replies, like nothing so much as sex. Sex in the bare earth under the oak trees. They smell of male sex. The trouble is I find them one after another after another and I don't get laid. By the end of a truffling day you hate their smell; it's as bad as working in a strip-joint. What's more, if you're not sharp, your nose gets scratched.

I sit beside Vico and watch him.

The other Vico, who was called Giambattista and lived two hundred and fifty years ago, apparently wrote a book called *The New Science*. When he finished it, nobody wanted to print it. So in 1725 he sold the only ring he possessed to pay the printer to publish it. It was a diamond ring and the diamond weighed five grams. Maybe this Giambattista didn't exist and Vico made him up.

Vico told me too that there are thousands of Vicos in Italy. The name is always placed in front of another one for it means "little street." Vico Garibaldi. In the summer most vicos have old women sitting in them, washing hanging out to dry, and young unemployed men taking turns going round the block on a clapped-out scooter. In most vicos during the winter there are only hungry cats and funeral notices.

Giambattista, Vico told me, wrote in Latin, a language which has disappeared. There was a Latin word *humanitas*, which meant the disposition of men to help one another. My ancestor, King, believed the word *humanitas* came from the verb *humare*, to bury. The burying of the dead is what he meant. Man's humanity, according to him, began with a respect for the dead. Yet you—you, King—bury bones too, don't you?

Vico started to laugh. He laughed so much he had to use his little finger to scratch his ear, which began to itch. His ears often itch when he laughs.

You bury bones too, don't you, King?

What with the laughter, the joke, and the itching ear, tears came into his eyes.

I'll tell you, King, my favourite quotation from my ancestor. "We wander," he wrote, "ignorant of the men and the places!" Imagine! He wrote that in his regular, modest house in Spaccanapoli two and a half centuries ago! And when he wrote it, he didn't imagine us!

I watch Vico in the doorway of the cut-price shoe shop, his eyes shut, his head nodding, his trouser bottoms rucked up so I can see the white of his legs, and I want to offer him something.

KING

A waterfall at a place called Haslach. The water came down in two swirls and as they fell, they plaited, the left one over the right and the right one under the left, and, behind them, a third stream of dark water fell straight.

If I can tell him about the three swirls of water, he'll fall asleep against the delivery door of the shoe shop.

Downstream there was a sandy beach, about the size of three cushions, and on the sand some stones had been deposited by the river. First large stones, which were embedded in the sand, and on top of them small stones, a handful, black or reddish in colour. The small stones rested where the large stones had little hollows—I could move them with my nose—yet each stone looked as if it had found the exact place in the world which had been made for it! If I tell him about these stones well enough, he won't feel the iron of the fucking door-bar sticking into his back.

When I stood there downstream from the waterfall, I knew that life, this bitch of a life, began when the first stone existed.

Men have seven skins. Water has five, and I can distinguish each one with my tongue. The first skin feels the wind, and however still the air, there's always a breath. The second skin feels only the temperature. On the third skin the current continually strokes the water the wrong way. The fourth is the wet skin, the fourth is really water. And the last skin? Through the last skin the minute mouths of minute fish filter light.

He is asleep now.

It's when I hear his butterfly voice speaking that I picture him young. Young, he has a proud, pronounced nose with flared nostrils—a nose which is going to take him far, a nose of intelligence. Every morning in Naples it smells the sea announcing the start of a day which is still fresh. At night he lifts it, so it is pointing to the stars above the bay.

Me, if I want to look at the sky, I have to do one of two things: either I put my head back, far far back, into the howling position, or I lie with my legs in the air in the position of surrender. From either of these two positions I can watch the stars and name the clouds.

This winter I found a new constellation. He's easy to find. You spot Scorpion and go to the opposite rim of the sky and you'll see Ram. If you come to Ram first and you're not sure, you can check whether Scorpion is on the opposite horizon. To the south of Ram there's Little Dog. Not the same as Hunting Dogs or Big Dog. To the north of Little Dog there's Goat and Giraffe, and between Goat and Little Dog to the east there's Castor and Lynx. Mule is in the centre of this triangle. His ears almost touch Castor. He stands above Ram, and like this he shelters him from the sun. From time to time Ram gets to his feet and scratches Mule's belly with his horns and Mule likes this.

They're bound together by an unbreakable friendship—Ram, who is there to mount as many ewes as the heavens bring him, and Mule, who can father nothing. Vico says I must have stolen stars from other houses to make Mule and that in fact he doesn't exist. Vica says she has seen Mule, no question, and of course he exists!

Today Vico's nose looks like a hammered piece of wood. I'm losing my sense of smell, he complained one evening to Vica when the three of us were walking back to Saint Valéry. Wait before you say that, Vica said, wait until I cook you my stuffed cabbage, you must cut it up with your knife so it soaks up all its juice, and we'll see then whether you've lost your sense of smell.

Once Vico had the nose of a man who could become rich. There are noses which can never emerge from poverty, the backstreet noses which I love licking and whose mouths call me every name under the sun. His nose was different: it was distinguished.

So was his forehead. Now his forehead is imprinted with screeching lines and skid marks showing what happened during the crash. Before, when he drew his inventions on a drawing board (if he's telling the truth), his forehead was like one of the city's domes, and girls tried to touch it with their long-nailed fingers because it promised patience and power. He mentioned to me once a girl called Valeria and as he did so he kept rubbing one of his own scaly fingers across his forehead as if trying to erase the skid marks for her. She played tennis, he said, and wore tall white socks . . .

He never snores. This is because, unlike Vica, he keeps his mouth shut when asleep. His tongue has gone into retreat. I have too much respect for him to say much about these things. Yet I cannot help imagining his tongue as it was before: eating melons, licking envelopes, tasting fish on the beach, looking for Vica's tongue, falling about in laughter.

Mouth shut, eyes shut, door shut on his face. I get to my legs, walk over, and lick his cheek.

He opens one eye, his right one, which is the joker eye, and in its surprise, at this moment between sleeping and waking, with the fucking iron bar in his back not yet recalled, for a second, in its surprise, I see the hope which used to be in it.

He opens both eyes and fingers the collar of his shirt.

King, he murmurs, so you got here. Let's go home.

We have to wait for Vica, I tell him.

I was trying to forget.

Yes, but we have to wait for Vica.

Some days I succeed, King, and when I do, it doesn't bring the relief I thought it would. I forget the past, and something else comes into my head which is as bad and, since I'm not used to it, it feels worse. I forget and I don't question myself any more about what I did or didn't do five years ago. I stop asking myself why I wasn't more attentive about the fire insurance. I stop wondering why I didn't listen to the last warning, the very last one. I let the past go, and it goes, and in its place comes the next hour. The next hour, King!

I say nothing. What can I say?

Yes, the next hour. It takes the place of the past. The next hour weighs nothing, it carries nothing, it has no documents, no names and addresses, no telephone numbers, it simply waits. And me, I know already I'm not going to do in the next hour what has to be done. I have to put an end to that hour. By putting an end to it, I finally sign the failure with my name.

And I know I'm not going to, King. I'm incapable, within the next hour, of ending anything. This is the worst. The failure goes away just like the past has done, it goes away unsigned. And I'm left with nothing. Absolutely nothing. The clock tells me an hour has passed. The next hour is another one, waiting. And I have nothing, nothing, nothing.

He strokes my head for the comfort when he repeats the word NOTHING.

No, it's not true.

How not true?

Fortunate Vico! I tease him.

Leave me alone.

We have the Hut and we have Vica.

Why don't you say YOU.

Me?

Count me out, he says.

Even when he is desperate, his voice is light, as if it were reading the words it says from a book written long ago.

On the other side of Sallust, above the hairdressers', I spot a new dog painting. The dogs must have climbed onto the roof of a van to spray so high. It's painted blue and white and shows a

wave breaking. Around the water are written the curling-up for-
nicating letters of the word WRACK.

Vico's hand is now pressing on my haunches and the pressure
I feel there has all the weight his voice lacks.

Time passes, he is saying, and nine times out of ten time
passing makes things worse! It's not true for civilizations or for
knowledge, but it's true for any body that is alone. Even the
earthworm's body. When time heals, it heals to draw out the
pain, to make it longer. There's no way back, and, each day, with
time passing, the way back is longer. This is what I think in the
morning when I go out of the Hut to piss.

If I thought the same every time I pissed!

We're a day further off, I say to myself. Now, without me,
Vica could still go back. She'd find a way. A little longer and
maybe she couldn't go back, she could today. She should leave.

I have a fisherman friend, I tell him, whose name is Anders,
and he has a boat called the *Galena*. Why don't you both go out
with him for a day? You and Vica.

You should leave me and take her back! he says.

The winter's over, I remind him, no more damp for six months,
and I've found you a boat for a cruise.

How shortsighted can a dog get?

Some dogs go blind, and others lead the blind, I say.

KING

A motorcycle messenger has stopped to buy an Orangina at the Pizza Hut. Helmet off, sitting astride the bike, he pours the juice down his throat and it washes away the dirt, and its coldness puts a sweet hand on his fatigue. Orangina.

What did you say? asks Vico.

I said, Orangina for the messenger.

You're wandering, King, wandering out of your mind.

There's a blind dog I know called Matthieu. He's old, a good bit older than you.

Nothing is older than me, says Vico.

His master is very methodical, I continue, his master learnt Method—how one thing leads to another—during years in a Kolyma prison camp, clearing forests. After he was liberated, he came home to his mother who was living with a pup called Matthieu. Years later the mother died and Matthieu grew old and went blind.

The guy never got married?

He says he couldn't organize a space for two, he's like a hermit crab. Consequence of the Gulag.

Russian?

Russian. He takes Matthieu for a walk every day, feeds him well, and when it's sunny sits in the garden with him. They talk a lot. Matthieu now knows a lot about the camps.

He's rich?

No, he's poor. Sometimes he goes out for the night to drink with friends. If it's winter, he leaves Matthieu on a blanket by the stove, and if it's summer, he leaves him on the terrace under the vine with the door open.

He sounds rich.

Compared to us he sounds well-off, but he isn't. Wherever it is that he leaves the dog, before he goes out for the night, he lays down on the floor a road of newspapers. And the road leads to the plate with Matthieu's food on it and a bowl of water. Like this the blind dog has only to follow the road with his paws.

Why can't he follow his nose?

His nose is blind too.

I say no more. We listen to the 38 tram coming down the street.

What's the Russian's name?

Vadim.

It's a story about newspapers?

About a man and a dog.

The sound of the 38 tram has gone.

After a long pause Vico says, Of course, the Hut means a lot to me. I don't forget when you and I were on the street. I don't forget. When I'm dead, I'll remember the Hut and forget all the other places I've lived in. Already they are becoming like hotels in my memory, nobody remembers hotels for long—except painters. They remember hotels. I don't know why.

Dog painters?

I had a painting of a hotel bedroom. By de Plessis. There was an oval mirror in the bedroom and lace pillows, and the head of the bed had brass globes which screwed off.

How do you know they screwed off if it was only a painting?

You care nothing about art, King, and not much about memory.

At memory I could beat you every time.

Where's Vica?

She's coming. She's not far away.

You sure?

I put my nose up in the air to convince him.

You'd be lost without her, wouldn't you? Vico says to me. Take her back whilst there's still time. Vica loved that de Plessis painting of a hotel bedroom. I bought it in Rome and I hung it in our office apartment in Zurich. It was the time of the Gore-Tex boom. A throw-off from the space program. The Gore-Tex membrane is made of two different polymers—polytetrafluoroethylene (e.PTFE), which is hydrophobic, and another polymer which is oleophobic. The e.PTFE membrane contains nine billion pores per square inch.

A girl from the hairdressers' on the opposite side of the street has come out on the sidewalk in her pale blue overall to smoke a cigarette. I relax because Vico is lost in his memories. When he talks like this his nose hides his mouth and he becomes almost inaudible. If I go and piss, he won't notice.

When I come back he's still in Zurich.

There was a stove covered in tiles which went up to the ceiling, and painted on the tiles were tulips. Niphetos tulips, for their petals had ragged edges. Vica and I moved in there five days after we met.

You weren't married then?

No.

You were never married?

No.

After two nos, I don't ask any more, even if at other times I lick his eyelids. No here means: Drop it!

Vica and I could see the lake from the bedroom window, he murmurs. The stove was built into the wall which divided the bedroom from the living room. It must have dated from the fin de siècle.

That's where we are now, isn't it?

The last one. You have no sense of history, King. The rooms were small and from the bed we could clearly see the tulips painted on the tiles. Painted in blue they were. Niphetos tulips with ragged petals.

I notice that the hairdresser girl across the street has gone in.

One morning I was half asleep—we Neapolitans need coffee in the morning and the Dutch are different, anyway Vica was different—one morning she got up to make the coffee and when she came back with it, before she'd drunk a drop, she made me a speech about tulips.

What did she say? I ask. In my opinion, a happy memory protects more than it rubs salt into the wound.

She said tulips come from Holland and the postcards were crap. I told her I thought they came from Turkey. I'm talking about now, she said, you have to look at one tulip, she said and you have to look at her every hour! All tulips are women, no exceptions. Men are begonias, dandelions, narcissi, anything you want but not tulips. Look at a tulip every hour, Gianni, and you'll see how she opens and shuts. Like an eye!

She didn't call you Vico then?

He ignored the question.

All flowers open and shut but tulips have their own way, she said. They have six petals like we have two arms, two legs, a torso and a head. Shut your eyes, Gianni, and imagine.

Leaning against the shoe shop delivery door, with my head on his thigh, which is as thin as a normal man's arm, Vico closes his eyes.

Two petals come together in the middle and make a purse, she explained. The four other petals cup round it, shoulders overlapping. When a tulip is shut, it's bulletproof, Gianni. Nothing in the world is more closed than a closed tulip and nothing can open her against her will. You can trample on her, you can tear her apart, you can destroy her in a second, but you won't have an open tulip, you'll have a victim, you'll have made something you don't want to look at. This is what she said.

Why did she call you Gianni?

Sitting on the bed, she looked at me and said, That's not the only thing. When a tulip opens of her own accord, her six petals bend back. The two who made the purse now open their arms to the sky, and the other four bend back so far that their hands, stretched above their heads, touch the floor! Like this! And throwing off her peignoir, she showed me, her whole wonderful body arched.

Why did she call you Gianni?

Because that was my name.

The two of us watch the feet passing along Sallust Street. Every street has a black hole you can fall down, and all the holes in all the streets of the world join in the same blackness, where there is everything and it seems like nothing.

She could still make it, if you took her back, Vico says.

Look at me! I say. I'm in no better shape than you. How can I take her back?

You know the road between things.

Things here I can lead somebody through, but for what you're asking you need papers and I have none.

More than papers you need what I haven't got any more, and you still have. It's why people talk to you. Even me. Do you know why people talk to you? They want to shock you. And you're not shocked, so they go on talking. You've seen everything and you're crazy enough to want to go on. This is why you have to take Vica back.

I'm not leaving you.

There's nothing to leave—some unsold radishes.

Vica is right, I say, you ought to be grateful.

When I'm dead I'll be grateful. I'll remember the Hut with gratitude. The Hut is the best thing I've had in my life. In the Hut the three of us are inside. It's inestimable, being inside. I come from Naples whose foundations are Greek and whose temples are Roman and I'm telling you without equivocation that the Hut in Saint Valéry is the best thing I've had in my life. Is that enough?

I've never heard anybody talk like you do, I tell him.

Of course not, I'm not talking.

Not talking?

You are listening. Nothing else is happening. Nothing else at all. Look at my lips, they are not moving, are they? The Hut is the best thing I've had in my life. The trouble is that I have to live in it and I have no reason for living.

You have the Hut.

I have to live in it.

Yes.

It's over, he says.

Only God can help. I tell him this with my eyes.

There are places God doesn't come to.

The terrain?

No. Here. He points his finger like a gun at his own temple.

Vica is coming! I tell him quickly.

Can you see her? he asks.

No.

KING

Where is she?

She's walking between the trees. Her name is in the air.

I can't see her, he says.

What will you say to her? I ask him.

You were a long time coming, I will tell her, but you've come!

I lit a candle! she'll say.

Both Vico and I know this will be her way of saying she drank a can of beer.

She arrives and sits down beside the box of unsold radishes and leans her back against the delivery door of the cut-price shoe shop. The three of us sigh as if we had had a narrow escape and, reunited at last, each of us can relax. Nobody speaks.

One of the things I most like doing is staying still.

After several centuries Vica says, My feet ache.

5:30 P.M.

Red, Vico told me one day, is the colour of sacrifice.

Really?

Both pain and triumph, he said, are in the colour red, and of course blood.

Blood isn't a colour, it's a taste, I growled.

Some reds are killing, others are healing, he went on. The abattoir and the geranium, King.

Sometimes I'm sorry for Vica; sometimes I believe Vico has gone mad.

Geraniums smell of wet silver, I said to tease him, go and sniff them in the cement coffins by the traffic light.

Then I felt ashamed of thinking him mad. Everyone at Saint Valéry needs a madness to find their balance after the wreck. It's like walking with a stick. Madness is the third leg. Me, for instance, I believe I'm a dog. Here nobody knows the truth.

Vico was talking about the colour red because of the Pizza Hut beside us on Sallust Street. Its uniforms are red, its shop front is red, its satchels for carrying the pizzas in are red, its logo, which hangs from a metal frame with feet on the pavement and which the sea wind blows so that it falls over like a talking drunk, is red, its bikes are red, its money bags are red, its telephones are red.

I've told you already about the Pizza Hut. I see it all the while. It doesn't go away. So I tell you again. They never offer us anything although we are in the next doorway. There's no waste in red Pizza Huts. The cheapest pizza there is the Margherita.

The Margherita was a Neapolitan creation, King, first made in 1830 for Marguerite de Savoie to convey to her excellency the loyalty of our city. It has the same colours as the national flag: red for pomodori, green for basilica, white for mozzarella!

I fix my eyes on the two of them sitting on the scraps of cardboard they bring in the chariot to sit on, so that the pavement is a little less cold and a little less rough with the dirt no one else notices, I fix my eyes on the two of them sitting on their cardboard with their backs against the doorway of the shoe shop. They are sitting close together, casually, unthinkingly, as only the intimate can do. And about neither of them can you suppose anything conclusive. Although they come here every day, their being here looks like an accident. Yet it's a choice, a reply to a question.

The two of them could stay in Saint Valéry. Why do they come to Sallust? To sell chestnuts and maize. To whistle up money if Vica is alone. Yet why do they come every day? Their coming is a way of replying no.

They're not going to get rid of us as easily as that! Vica told Vico one morning when he didn't want to get out of bed.

What difference does it make?

We can't hide here, she said, all day in the Hut. Are you ill?

No, I'm not ill.

We'll go together, my love, and take King, she said.

I look along the street. It runs gently uphill. It's not steep, but a man operating a wheelchair by himself would feel it in his arms. The buildings are three storeys high and the bay windows of all the front rooms jut well out over the sidewalk, as if the apartments were waiting for a giant to transport them elsewhere in the night, and this is to give his fingers the chance of getting a firm grip under the first floor so as to be able to lift up everything above the shops in one go, and take the two upper floors to a happier place. At the top of the rise the tram lines disappear and the street runs steeply downhill so you see no traffic and no people, only the faraway, hazy districts with the office blocks half finished and abandoned. It's when I look into this distance, head on my paws, that I think: Where does it stop?

Malak showed me a gold ring which Liberto gave her. When he nicked it, she said, he didn't know what he'd got, it was I who discovered its secret. On the inside of the ring was a hard white metal, not gold, and into this metal some words were engraved. I couldn't read them. They were too small and they were in reverse. You'd need a mirror. So I put the ring on my finger, King, it was tight, I had to use soap. Now watch! I'm going to take it off for you. Wait. There! What's written on the skin of my finger? FORGET ME NOT. Those three words printed all round my finger. Imagine it. You can lick my finger, King, lick it, and they won't come off!

Maybe it's the same with the three bridges over the river near my beach. They print FORGET ME NOT on the water. Except when the night is utterly black.

Suddenly Vica shouts, You wouldn't be able to sell a bottle of Schweppes tonic in the desert!

The pitch of her voice makes me think she has had at least two cans of beer.

You can't sell anything!

I recognise the voice. It is the voice which believes, against all the odds, that it can joke about everything.

You take off your cap for me and lay it down on the pavement, the voice orders.

Vico's eyes are sadder than mine can ever be. He too recognises the voice.

You know what I'm going to do? the voice says, I'm going to sing.

No, Vica, you're tired.

I'm not tired.

Then I am.

You used to tell me I had a golden voice, you don't like my voice any more?

Not here, Vica, this is all I ask, not here.

I'm going to sing the *Qui la voce* aria from *I Puritani*. I know I haven't got Callas's voice.

Not any more, no.

If you'd sold the radishes, I wouldn't have to, would I? Take your cap off and put it on the pavement and we'll try Bellini.

She's waiting for us to laugh and we don't. She picks up one of the unsold bunches and starts to nibble a radish. I'm hungry, she says. She holds another radish out to Vico, who shakes his head. Then she hurls the whole bunch back into the cardboard box.

I'm waiting for the cap.

Not now.

Why not?

I ask you not to, Vica.

I enjoy singing, I've always enjoyed singing.

Another day, not today.

We'll go home with some money if I sing.

I don't think so.

When I'm not with you I sing—ask him!

She nods at me. I get to my feet and go and stand with my head on her shoulder. Sometimes she sings, it's true, and sometimes somebody searches for a coin to give her, but nobody listens to her. Vica is not like Alfonso. She climbs onto the music in her head, as if it were a tram she's catching. Nobody realises she is singing for them. Alfonso watches all the while—watches for the pigs and also for the smiles. His eyes say: I'm singing the song you want to hear, aren't I? We were all there together, remember? And everybody puts a hand in their pocket. Poor Vica shuts her eyes and travels alone on the tram to its terminus.

You were right about the radishes, says Vico, I was unable to sell them. The maize goes well, it's a man's product.

Are you ashamed of my voice, is that what you mean?

You have a beautiful voice, Vica.

(Here is a list of the other objects in the two-litre jar on the iron stove in Saint Valéry, the definitive list of Vica's and Vico's private treasures: a walnut, a champagne cork, an Alfa Romeo key ring, a plastic bag of red sand, a white ribbon, a cameo photo of Vica as a baby, a wine-coloured hairnet, a statuette of Saint Janvier which belonged to Vico's mother—and a postcard from Pozzuoli with the word ZIZZA written on it in Vica's hand-writing. *Zizza* means tit.)

You are ashamed of me!

No. I'd be ashamed of your using your voice—

If I was younger, Vico, can you guess what I'd use?

Don't!

We could both live off it. You can guess, can't you?

Let's go home.

With difficulty Vico gets to his feet and grasps the chariot.

When we were sleeping in the street and Vica wasn't yet with us, Vico told me one night about his first invention. It was long before I had the factory, King, I was seventeen. I had an uncle who suffered from multiple sclerosis. He couldn't do anything with his hands or legs. He could only listen and observe and talk.

KING

He often talked to me. He lived with my aunt, his sister, in the Spaccanapoli district. She worked as a seamstress. They were poor. His passion was listening to the radio. He knew everything about what was happening in the world, and it was he who first persuaded me to read Giambattista. Yet he couldn't change the stations for himself, he couldn't use his hands. He had to interrupt his sister and ask her to come over to the radio and turn the knob. And this meant she had to stop working. So he often listened to what didn't interest him to save interrupting his sister. After he told me this, I took a look at the radio and its tuner. I did some drawings. And I invented a tuner he could operate with his nose!

We'd be in the money, Vica screams, and you'd soon get used to it, if I was forty years younger!

I beg you, Vica—

I'd carry on every night till four in the morning, and I'd take the last client at three!

Please stop . . .

You waited too long before you lost everything, Vico, you should have done it when I was younger, then I could have helped you with more than my voice!

Get back to Holland, Vico shouts, and take King with you. Get back to your brother in Amsterdam.

Brother!

He'll be obliged to take you in. Get back. Get back whilst there's still time. Leave me.

You waited too long! she screams.

Both of them are now on their feet, bawling at each other, and the passersby edge away in disgust and alarm.

The passersby see three more plague victims. Deep down everybody knows that nobody is telling the truth about this plague. Nobody knows whom it selects and how. And so everywhere there is a fear of infection.

When the Plague struck Naples in 1656, King, seven out of every ten people died.

The sight we offer, the three of us—an old man, an old woman, and their dog in a delivery doorway screeching at each other and standing on pieces of cardboard, hands grubby and swollen, eyes misty, making no effort to improve their lot, indifferent to hope and reasoning—this sight is disgusting and infectious. It saps confidence, and a lack of confidence diminishes immunity.

Flush them out, mutters a man with a telephone in his hand, they should be hosed off the street. As he passes, he kicks at me.

I'm not leaving you, Vica says, panting.

Without me you'll survive, Vico replies.

No.

KING

Leave me the chariot and take King. Start tonight, he says.

Never.

There's nothing nothing nothing for you to stay for. You said so yourself.

I never said such a thing, for Christ's sake I didn't. I just said take your cap off so I can sing.

I don't want you to sing.

Vica begins to cry. Small tears roll down either side of her nose. She sits down and leans back against the delivery door. So does he. Their shoulders touch. I try to lick her face and she pushes me away. Vico looks at his watch.

I'm not going to do in the next hour what has to be done, he says.

Vica sobs quietly.

Let's sleep a moment, I say.

She leans her head against his shoulder.

We should start, he says, it'll be dark in two hours.

I have a torch, she says with her eyes shut.

I watch the ankles of the passersby. Men's. Women's. In trousers, in tights, bare. They wear Reeboks, platform shoes, sneakers, tall boots. The offices are closing, their screens shut down. The sides of all the shoes are a little nearer to the ankle than this morning, a wafer nearer. Everybody is taller when going to work, shorter when going home.

Both have their eyes shut. The clouds in the sky are crossing the street. In this city by the sea all the clouds are torn by the wind. They are never here to stay; every cloud is leaving. Cirrus spissatus. Altocumulus lenticularis.

Five minutes and we go, announces Vico without opening his eyes.

I remember Jack's message, which I haven't delivered to them.

He wants everybody back early, I say.

Who? asks Vico, his eyes still shut.

Jack the Baron.

Why? asks Vica.

He's got problems, I say.

Did you wait for him?

Vica's question is so stupid I pretend not to hear it. All the time she makes you run back to her. With Vico you can trot side by side.

Did he get to the City Hall? she asks.

KING

His coat was torn, I say.

I loved his coat this morning, she says.

Four minutes and we go, announces Vico.

I hear the drone of a pizza bike, high-pitched as an enraged bee. Bees are the other creatures who, like us, are specialists concerning fear. They sting fear.

The rider shoves his front wheel into the slot of the parking stand and at the same time kills the motor. I don't have to open an eye to know what he's doing. It's routine. He'll take off his red helmet, open the red box on the back of the bike, the box which is large enough to carry eight Mega Cheezy Crusts, and he'll take out his red satchel and go into the shop to see whether there's another delivery order. It's early yet. The last order was for four sailors just come ashore.

I can tell from their breathing that they're asleep. Cats pass where their whiskers can pass. With us it's our ears. I speak of these things so as not to think of others.

Danger! Very near danger. A klaxon and the slithering rumble of a wall falling, which is the noise a heavily loaded twenty-five-ton lorry makes when desperately braking to a standstill. Before I know it, I'm on my four feet, watching, coat bristling. And what do I see?

The lorry that braked is on the far side of the street. The driver is furiously pumping a fist up and down in the air. On this side of the street several cars and a van and a taxi have stopped. Everything is waiting. A tram is coming down the hill.

In the middle of the street—she has just passed the lorry, which, like its driver, is still shuddering—skips the girl from the hairdressers', the girl who came out for a smoke, the girl with nails the colour of black currants. She no longer has an overall on. She's wearing a very short blue dress with wisps of white like the sky with its torn clouds. She is skipping and running and laughing, her arms stretched out, her thumbs up, her fingers apart, her hair brushed back from her ears, and she is splicing the air of Sallust on her way to the red bike stand beside us.

By the bike stand, a rider with his red tunic undone, hair to his shoulders, his head thrown back, drinks water from a bottle. He knows she's arriving. He's cooling his mouth for her.

He takes a slow step to the curb and raises his arms and she flings herself into them. Her hands with the black-currant fingernails grasp the rungs of his back. The lorry driver smiles and makes another gesture—the gesture of a man picking fruit. He lets out the clutch and the lorry with its sixteen wheels unrolls towards Berlin.

King, whispers Vica, come here, I have something to tell you. Quietly, don't wake him up.

You saw her stop the traffic? I ask her.

No, it was him.

He was on the sidewalk all the while, I say, like a piece of dog shit.

It was him! she insists, raising the voice.

You must have had your eyes shut, I tell her, you must have dropped off, it was she who stopped the traffic.

She couldn't have done it without him, that's what I'm saying.

He wasn't even looking.

He was there! That's what matters, says the voice raised still higher.

And now they're kissing, I say.

He was there, she goes on in the raised voice. And his being there made all the difference! She saw him standing there. There, where before there was nobody at all. It wasn't even an empty space like an empty seat. There was no room for anybody, it was goddamned everlasting Sallust . . . and suddenly he was there.

The reckless voice now changes to a murmur: She comes out of the hairdressers', King, she's finished her day's work. She changes her shoes, you can't wear high heels when you're on your feet all day doing hair. She comes out of the shop and she glances across the street at the Pizza Hut, she's met a couple of his mates there in their red helmets and she didn't like them, she thought they were fucked up—and he's the last person she's expecting to see at this moment, they have their rendezvous in two hours' time, and he's there! He's there, King, sitting on his moped in his red jacket, head back, drinking from a bottle. She's going to run to him. If he's there, she whoops to herself, the traffic can't kill me today! She steps straight off the sidewalk without waiting. You don't do that if you haven't said to yourself: The traffic can't kill me today! She steps off the sidewalk into the road, laughing, and the traffic stops for her.

They're kissing now, I say again.

The traffic can't kill me today, Vica repeats to herself, because he's there, because he's there!

I can see the hairdresser girl is familiar with his mouth, she knows where to go, and she's touching his eyelid with one of her fingers.

I'm going to tell you something now, King. A long time ago I was as young as her. I was staying with my friend Saskia. Saskia was married to an optician in Zurich. And I was doing one term in the Conservatoire there. My feet were tiny in those days and I was wearing a pair of white sandals. You can't imagine what I was like then, King. It's not that I was very beautiful. I was so fresh, so healthy. I think I glistened. And I was walking by the lake alone, licking an ice cream. The month of August, a hot and heavy afternoon. It started to rain. The rain fell so hard it tore the leaves off the trees and when the raindrops hit the lake, the lake spat back, like oil in a pan when you drop in the chips. I had a cotton dress on. I still remember it. A very dark green, like laurel. The laurel leaf green went well with my long straight blond hair. So when the rain started, I ran across the street to the nearest doorway, holding a glossy magazine above my head, and there in the doorway I went on licking my ice cream. I didn't know about ice creams then. For me, then, certain ice creams were coated with chocolate, some weren't, and then there were water ices, that's all I knew. It was he who was going to teach me about ice creams in Naples, but he wasn't there yet. How could a Dutch girl in those days know about ice creams?

The only Dutch girl I ever met was in a lorry going to Hamburg, I tell her with my eyes. At night she fucked with the driver in the back of the lorry.

Licking my ice cream, I saw a man holding a dispatch case over his head and he was running through the rain like somebody dribbling a ball at his feet. At first I wanted to laugh. I think I did laugh. He was so much on his toes. Then I saw he was running to the shelter of the same doorway I was standing in. He installed himself beside me, placed his dispatch case on the ground, brushed each wet shoulder with his other hand, adjusted a button of his white shirt, and mildly shook the water off his head—like you do sometimes. After all that, he turned to me.

Handsome?

What's handsome, Handsome? She fingers my ear.

Did you want to go with him?

I didn't know him. He didn't concern me. He was well dressed. I thought he might be Italian because of the way he ran, as if he was dribbling a ball at his feet. He wasn't a man you could trip up easily, I saw that much. Of course I wasn't thinking of going with him. And there are no two women who agree about what makes a man handsome. It's not a thing you can measure. And anyway it changes, doesn't it? It comes and it goes. It goes.

I make a point of not looking at Vico. Vica, if need be, would slit a throat. She would screw up her eyes afterwards but she'd do it if it had to be done. Not him. He couldn't. The most he might do is blow out his own brains.

With a Beretta? she whispers. I never knew Vica could read my thoughts to this point.

He used to carry one, she says, smiling, when he was being threatened by the Camorra. You're right, he would never have used it, but he told everyone and he took it out of his pocket to show them, so it protected him in another way. It was a chrome Beretta. They once said they'd close down his factory if he didn't pay. His factory in those days was on the Riviera di Chiaia.

Vico, now asleep on the pavement, puts his fist up to his mouth like babies do when sleeping.

What did he say? I ask.

He said no, under no circumstances.

What did he say in Zurich? What did he say to you that first time in the doorway?

He said nothing. Vico has never been one of those men who talk because they're nervous. I didn't say anything either. He had such assurance. Not in his head—it wasn't conceit. His assurance was in his feet, in his body, like an animal.

Me for example.

Not like you, you're scared all the while. You have no confidence, King, let's face it. He was like a deer. Maybe deer are stupid but they have assurance. You can see it in the way they stand—they seem to have been made, from hoof to antler, without a second's hesitation. He was standing beside me like that, and I looked back at him, very calm. There were still drops of rain running down his long nose. At last he spoke: So we've both swum ashore! The two of us. My name is Gianni. Do tell me your name. He spoke in a funny way—like he was reading a libretto, and he spoke German with an Italian accent, as if he had to do Wagner but preferred Verdi, though I didn't know then how much he loved opera, I didn't know anything about him. He was there, that's all. And I said to myself: The traffic can't kill me today.

His voice when I met him was the first thing I noticed too, I tell Vica.

He wasn't the same man by the time you met him, King.

He had the same voice.

That is what is terrible about voices, she says.

What next? I ask.

He invited me for coffee. I asked him what he did. He said he was an inventor.

Did he tell you about his uncle?

No, he told me about his factory and he told me my dress was most beautiful. He said there was a painting called *The Thunder*

Storm in which there was a green landscape exactly like the green of my dress.

By Giorgione.

How the hell do you know?

He told me.

What hasn't he told you?

He hasn't told me what he has forgotten.

She begins to dab at her eyes.

I've forgotten nothing, she says. I saw him every day and then he had to go back to Italy to his factory. I wondered whether he was married.

He wasn't.

I know, but then I didn't quite believe him.

And the next month when he came back to Zurich, you moved into his flat?

You know too much, King, too much to be good for you, that's why you are scared all the while.

In his flat there was a tiled stove and the tiles had tulips on them?

No.

That's what he told me.

There were no tiles with tulips.

Never mind, I say.

When did he tell you about the tulips?

I don't remember.

It was I who bought the tiles with tulips later, Vica says, as a surprise for him.

Okay. Sooner, later, it doesn't matter, he loved the tulips, I tell her.

This is a list of the places where I prefer to rest my head. On Vico, below his last rib near the solar plexus, or beside his neck with his collarbone under my jaw. On Vica my favourite places are between her belly and the top of her thighs when she's sitting, the small of her back when she is sprawled on her front, and the side of her head when she's asleep. I put my head now on the top of her thighs and listen.

Most smiles promise too much, have you noticed that, King? You're bound to suspect them, you back away, don't you? Most smiles are made to deceive. Vico's smile promised nothing. Nothing. So I loved it, and I didn't think twice about loving it. His smile meant he had all he wanted at the moment. I could put my finger between his teeth. It also meant that if I was threatened, he'd jump at the throat of whatever was threatening me.

He was like nothing I had seen before. He was like everything I had not seen and knew I had not seen. So he was familiar to me, and unheard of. He didn't make any promises. And I wouldn't have believed him if he had.

I sigh or I bark without knowing it, softly. There are barks so soft they stay under the tongue. The hairdresser girl in the sky-blue dress takes her mouth off the Pizza Hut boy's mouth and turns her head to look at me because she heard me sigh.

Is he young? she asks.

He's not old like me, screeches Vica.

You're only young once, the girl says.

No, replies Vica in the screech voice, you're young a million times, you're young a million million times, and afterwards they seem like only once.

How old is he?

I wouldn't know. My husband doesn't know either. None of our neighbours know. He turned up eighteen months ago.

Not long.

An eternity! Vica screeches. An eternity here . . .

What's his name? asks the Pizza Hut boy, who can't see anything except the girl's hair, which is over his eyes and which smells of skin, her skin and nobody else's. What's he called?

We call him King. Before—he must have had another name. Things are simpler if you take a new name, so we call him King. We call you King, don't we?

He's intelligent, says the Pizza Hut boy, you can see that by the way he's listening to us.

I like your bloke's voice, says Vica to the girl, you can tell a lot about a man from his voice.

Lovely tall mouth, the girl whispers to the Pizza Hut boy, giving his lips a lick.

Vica goes on: Today the traffic can't kill me—that's what you said this afternoon, isn't it, sweetie, when you tore across the street?

Going to get a job as a long-distance driver, the boy says, I'll need a dog.

I'm not letting him go away, the girl says, I want to move to the country and I'll do hairdressing in people's homes, there's a steady trade in the countryside because of all the weddings and first communions and funerals. Isn't that right, lady?

I have the key to a house, says the boy.

Far? I ask.

I'm not telling anybody where it is yet, not even her.

Hairdresser and Pizza Hut boy disengage. She relaxes the knee and thigh of her leg which was pressing upwards between his two, she gently lowers her chin so her ears come forward, and she lets go of the rung of his back, whilst he, firmly holding her where she is by her hips, takes a step back. Then they smile at each other like two loaves just come out of the same oven. He slips the red strap off his shoulder—he's finished work—and she busies herself adjusting the buttons of his shirt with her black-currant fingernails.

You're right, the traffic can't kill me today, lady! she whispers to Vica as she goes hand in hand with her bloke into the Pizza Hut.

Do you know where men are really different from women, King, not where you think, there the things are just tied up differently, different ribbons, no, where the real difference is, is here by the shoulders, what I call a man's roof—this sloping bit from the shoulders to the chest. Why do all the statues which don't have any heads or arms or pricks or feet still look like men, unmistakably men? It's all to do with what happens here, with the dear roof. From one of the windows in the flat we could see the Zürichsee. In each of his shoulders there were four swellings which were hard or soft as he chose to make them. I used to hold them. I played with them, I put my cheek against them, I gave them names. One I called Strength, another I called Prudence, and then there was Justice. I forget the fourth for the moment, forgive me, King. He laughed when I told him about the names and said I was a hopeless Calvinist. Which perhaps I was then, but not later. Very soon I wasn't Calvinist. Which doesn't stop the beauty of a man's body always having something to do with the upright, with standing upright.

There are plenty of crooked men, I mumble into her thigh.

At the back there are the shoulder blades and in front there's this roof, this roof made for two. Ask the hairdresser, King, she'd know what I'm talking about.

A man is most beautiful when he is on the point of walking forward, his belly fluttering like a tight curtain under the roof, on the point of advancing, his prick a dove behind the curtain, his arms, which are going to hold you, still hanging, warmer on the inside where they've touched his body, and his slim hips tucked under the roof, leaving you all the room you need all night long, whatever the weather. This is when he's most beautiful, King.

From each shoulder a little path ran down to his nipple. The little pip of a nipple which is there for nothing. I went down the path with my front teeth—they were white then, King.

He tapered down from his shoulders like a tree the wrong way up. So sometimes I lay with my feet by his ears, sucking his big toe, so I could put my arms round and measure him as if he was a tree.

An elderly man wearing a black hat with a large brim stops in front of us. He smells of clean clothes and age. Vica has her hand held out. She keeps it held out whilst she tells me all these things. Occasionally it falls, or she rubs her eyes with it, but most of the time it implores the passersby. They don't hear us talking. They merely see a large woman in blue jeans with a dog who has his head on her lap and behind the pair of them an old man asleep. The person in the black hat with a large brim chooses a twenty note from his purse, and stooping, with some difficulty, places it in her hand. Her hand closes discreetly in acknowledgement. She says nothing. With her other hand she makes a sign: the sign a mother makes at the school gates to encourage her child, who doesn't want to walk away from her, to go. The old man straightens up and, less displeased with himself than before, makes for the boulevard.

I believed him, King. Whenever I touched him, I believed him. Do we ever know how to say what we believe? When we can say it, it's no longer true, the belief has gone. I believed Life had led me to this man and the same Life had led him to being what he was. And what he was I could touch. I didn't listen too much to his words. I listened to his voice without hearing the words, and I touched him.

I believed we were going to live a life that would give things back to Life in exchange for the unheard-of chance of us two having met! I could never get used to how new he was. In the evening when he came back from work he was new. In the morning when he went to work he was new, very new. Today the traffic can't kill me, I told myself every morning. Even when I knew him by heart and my fingers were experts in every crease of his body, he was new. He was older than me, he had already lived a life and yet he was new.

With my tail I can thump Vico's leg, he's that close as he sprawls on the pavement. Everything she's telling me is somewhere in his eyes. And his eyes are shut. Sleep is best.

KING

I've been with other men, King, you know that, before him and after, and I've never felt the same thing. Other men do things. He just was.

I thump Vico's leg with my tail.

We're going to the opera! he said one night. There isn't an opera on in Zurich, I told him. I've booked, he says. *Il Trovatore*. La Scala, Milano! We're taking a sleeper tonight.

He had a way of taking decisions which kept me guessing—as if every decision he made was an envelope with a secret message inside, and when he made the decision he sealed the envelope before handing it to me. He loved nothing better than organising surprises. And when the surprise came, he loved to see me clap in delight.

Vica starts to clap her two hands and I put my nose between them to stop her. It is better he doesn't wake up yet. The longer she can talk after the beer the less chance of a fight between them.

What shall we give my mother for her birthday? he asked me. I don't know your mother, I said. I think we should give her you! And ecco! he pulls out of his pocket two air tickets to Naples.

We doused the fires for you, he said in the plane, there's Vesuvius, he's only smouldering now, drink your Campari! I kissed him. And we came down to land over the bay. His mother was a widow with black earrings who kept birds. She had six birdcages hanging from her windows on the second floor and the birds sung day and night.

Fortunately she died eight years ago, so she can't see where we are today. She thought I would have a steadying effect on her son. He sees so far some mornings he can't find his shoes! she told me one Sunday on the way to church. Mark my words, she went on, he'll change with age, I won't be here to see it, but mark my words, my son Gianni will change and you'll be beside him, won't you?

One night she whispered to me whilst I was washing my hair in the bathroom: You've come at the right time, mia coccolina, on Saturday you can go and see Nostra Madonna di Regnos Altos!

The Madonna was in the Spanish district, where everything was dirty except the washing. They wash their rags all the while. The houses were small, one room on each floor, and the streets were narrow and dark.

We're not far, Gianni said, from where Giambattista Vico lived, not far from the street where the first genius of modern thought was born! Do you know why he was the first genius of modern thought? He was the first thinker to see that God is powerless. When she heard this, his mother crossed herself three times.

Why am I telling you all this, King?

Because you know I'm listening to you.

It doesn't do an atom of good.

It brings us a little closer.

To what?

To what you and I don't know.

The narrow street is full of people moving, moving house, King. Men, women, children, so many in the narrow street that Gianni and I have to keep shifting ourselves. His mother has gone home. And the same is happening in the other streets which cross the one we are in. There is no corner which is calm. Everybody is leaving. The men are carrying on their backs bundles of cut rushes twice as tall as they are. The women are coming out of their doors with rolled carpets and folded linen and their lace and mirrors and candlesticks. And the children, who have found a van-load of empty cardboard boxes, are building towers with them. I don't know why. Is Vesuvius going to erupt? Have they received a warning to bring out their valuables and take them to a shelter somewhere else?

I'm not frightened because I'm with Gianni. He doesn't tell me anything. He leaves me guessing. He was often like that in those days. It was his way of encouraging me to learn things, and he'd watch with a teacher's smile, which would change into a smile of delight, for my innocence was also a mystery to him and he fed on it. When he watched me eating nocciole gelati, he remembered what it was like to eat a nocciola for the first time!

Men are carrying coloured lamps, stepladders, long poles. A man in a wheelchair is unwinding strings with sheets of coloured paper threaded on them, and the coloured papers have hearts and diamonds cut out of them. Over the cardboard towers built by the children, women are spreading cloths of velvet. Velvet is dream, velvet is night, velvet is welcome, velvet is a whore, velvet is love, King. On the velvet they place treasures which have been polished to shine.

Other men are planting the rushes as if they were trees, poking their stalks between paving stones and securing them with twine and batons, and, above, bending the trees towards each other so they touch, and stay touching by being tied, turning all the streets into aisles no wider than a man's two outstretched arms, and along the aisles people go walking like couples to an altar. Gianni and I too.

The streets are dressing up. All the streets will sing tonight. Some will get drunk. Others won't stop laughing. Some will dance, without stopping once. This street will sit down to eat all night like a man. This one will arrange marriages like a woman. And this one, which leads to a flight of steps, will wait for its sailors to come home.

Gianni takes me by the arm and says: You see the little window beside the front door? Yes? It opens outwards, and when somebody dies in this house they are brought out through the window, never through the door. They are overcrowded, these houses, because they are poor, so they don't want the dead coming back unexpectedly, slipping in whenever the front door is open! Like this, the dead have to tap on the window if they've forgotten something. Don't look so worried, nobody has died here for months. When there's a death, the street doesn't dress up for a whole year.

The old women are hanging lace on rough, stained, pissed-against walls, making the street white. Lace is luxury, lace is loneliness, lace is waiting, lace is fingering, lace is delicacy, lace is for the poor, lace is attention, lace is seduction. How proud they were, hanging their lace up in their street. They all knew which were the best pieces, even if they didn't say. Maybe they didn't know when they were young.

With bitter experience we all learn to judge lace.

By evening there are more flowers in the streets than when a king dies. Roses, lilies, giant daisies, almond blossom, asphodels, honeysuckle, hibiscus, syringa, apple blossom, and from the strung-up trees without roots hang garlands of laurel. And the coloured lights are alight with the colours of all the gelati in Naples: stracciatella, fragola, nocciola, tutti frutti, coccomero, albicocca, red cherries . . .

Vica is singing. She doesn't know she's singing. Vico doesn't hear her. We lie slumped in the delivery doorway. There's nothing to be heard at all, and she's singing to me.

Old men with veined hands, King, are protecting the flickering flames of the white candles, and in the centre of each display of candles a Madonna, who has been brought out of the house, makes a little silence whilst she waits.

All the Madonnas, King, are wearing blue and gold, some are wooden, most are in china, a few in porcelain. Everyone knows who is the richest, nobody knows who is the poorest. On the tables before the front doors are laid out sweetmeats, just baked in the little ovens: macaroon biscuits made from almonds, doughnuts the colour of brass covered in silver sugar, wafers the size of cats' tongues which taste of lemon, amoretti morbidi.

The little Madonnas are waiting for the tall Madonna di Regnos Altos to come down from the church on the hill to bless their houses. And when she comes she'll be wearing yellow roses.

Gianni takes my hand. Two carabinieri on motorcycles ride towards us at the speed of your Mule, trying to clear a way down the aisle of the street, which is already packed with little girls in their best dresses with ribbons, ribbons are bows, ribbons are plaits, ribbons are wrists, ribbons are for pulling, with fathers in ironed shirts and polished shoes and brushed hats, with old women who yesterday were doing each other's hair, with old men counting—they count the dead, the years, the Madonnas, the grandchildren, lire, the number of bottles waiting, the date of the next lottery—with mothers who will no longer be tired when they start to dance, and dance they will with whoever asks them, except Jacopo or Giorgio, and most carefree of all when they dance with each other, vast heaving bodies making them laugh as they recall the roll call at school: Rosa, Teresa, Paola, Lucietta, Matilda, Brigida.

How did they clear the street? I'll tell you, King. First the houses emptied themselves into the street, then the street, which felt entirely at home, emptied itself into the houses. All the doors are open.

Now comes the bandmaster walking backwards. I say to myself: Gianni will be like him when Gianni is old. The bandmaster must be in his late sixties yet he has the same lightness on his toes as Gianni, the same way of keeping his elbows high, the same authority, the same sense of rhythm. Yes, Gianni will be like him, and Gianni has a faultless ear, so when he retires he can teach music a little, why not? And he'll probably be bald like the bandmaster is.

Don't look at him now, King.

The band is filling the street with music until it overflows. It overflows into every cupboard and cellar and attic and stairway. The musicians' uniforms are red and black and the caps have white bands of rep. Thirty musicians of all ages.

What about the girls? I ask.

Look at them, King, they were ten years younger than I was then. They're bursting as they purse their lips around their mouthpieces, with their short skirts, smiling knees, up-to-date wedge shoes so cheeky they want to giggle, and the cheek comes from their knowing for certain, as they step slowly down the aisles, that the music on the music sheets at the end of their clarinets and flutes, all the flats and sharps and quavers and semi-quavers are there on their five lines to show off and shine on their youth, the notes are dancing under their skin without a word, and the bandsmen behind them, red-faced from blowing the tubas and bassoons, are flushed with pride as they serenade the girls in their last white socks, young enough to be their daughters.

The bandmaster lets his arm slowly fall and the music dies away. Gianni leads me to a low wall and tells me to stand on it. I'm here, he says to reassure me.

The bandsmen pass a bottle of water around between them. The chinaware Madonna, surrounded by her cushions and her

bottled pears from last year and her lit candles, stands there waiting. She is waiting for the tall one, Nostra Madonna di Regnos
Altos.

Standing on the wall, I remember from the Bible the miracle
of the seven loaves and little fishes which feed the multitude of
four thousand, and I watch the miracle of how many people the
little corner of the street makes room for, still leaving space for
the priest who walks down the aisle leading the tall Madonna,
decked out in her yellow roses and standing on a raft carried on
the shoulders of four men with arms like boxers.

The two of them face each other with no words at all, the tall
one with her smooth forehead and her long arms and the palms
of her hands facing forward, and the little one who stands all the
year on a shelf above the double bed in the small house. Between
the two of them there's a miraculous silence which fills the entire
street. I can hear the buzz of an electric plug for the wiring of the
coloured bulbs because it hasn't been pushed in as far as it should
be. Nothing else. The flowers in the vases are waiting and the
lace covers hung on the filthy walls and the men who cough, and
the tables and chairs in the rooms, and the plates and knives and
forks and spoons, the towels, the ironed shirts, the shoes, the
children's socks, the figs picked yesterday, and every room, filled
with silence, is waiting. I'm waiting and Gianni beside me is
waiting, and as I wait I think of the roof of his shoulders when I
stood in front of him without a stitch on.

The priest asks Nostra Madonna di Regnos Altos to bless this
abode and those who live in it and will live in it during the next
year, for ever and ever, amen.

The Madonna smiles as she was smiling before and as she's probably smiling now. And the street makes the sign of the cross across its narrow chest and the band reassembles and the children yell and the grandmothers hand round plates of sweetmeats and the men shout to one another, Coming tonight? Coming tonight? and the girls flick to the next page of their music and Gianni turns to me and says: And if I ask you to be Signora Vico?

Yes, I replied, yes.

So you are married?

I didn't say so. I said he asked me.

And you said yes.

He asked me many times and each time I cried with pleasure and said yes, King.

So why didn't you get married?

Who said we didn't?

You tell me what you want. Just what you want.

I wanted to tell you, King, about the first time and the blessing of the home, that's all.

She lets her head slump forward and soon her breathing changes. On the sea the sun is setting and is very near the horizon. From the doorway in Sallust I can't see the sea or the sunset, yet I know where the sun is by the colour of the clouds. They're asleep, both of them, wrapped in their coats.

When there's no more glow on the clouds, I'll wake them. To wake Vico I gently bite his knuckles. I've tried other ways: this is the one he prefers.

For Vica I'll pick up her hand in my mouth and go along her arm dropping and catching it in my mouth without ever a tooth grazing her until I reach the armpit.

Why don't you carry me home? she'll say.

I'll go back down her arm to the wrist.

We're lost, King.

And I'll let her arm fall.

8:00 P.M.

First there's Vico, then there's Vica pushing the chariot, and then me. We walk one behind the other. We have learnt that this is the best way to walk at night. Less tiring, safer, and quieter. Each of us walks with our own thoughts or with our own phrase for the evening, repeated again and again.

There's nothing, nothing for you to stay for.

Today the traffic can't kill me.

There are plenty of crooked men.

KING

The three phrases shuffle one behind the other.

There is a full moon in the southeast. As I bring up the rear I dream of a night when the poor are rich. I see my beach. The horizon has gone and the sea with it. There is only the sky, and the sky comes down to where the shingle stops and the rocks begin. The jetty is a jetty into the firmament. When I go to the wrack line to paddle, my paws paddle in the sky. I plunge my head into the icy infinity of the universe and, shaking it dry, I shake out stars.

Dogs should not dream. They should never dream. The hand of a man passing me on the sidewalk accidentally brushes against my ribs and a memory comes back, comes back so fast I can do nothing, and unlike the lorry for Berlin, it doesn't stop, it flattens me.

Long ago I was near an airport. There was a camp: canvas hangars, barbed wire, bunks, searchlights, prams being used as carts, chaos, people waiting, some alone, some with part of their families, all waiting interminably to return home, to go abroad, to be given something. They had nothing. I was there as a guard dog.

A woman calls me over to her. She tells me her name is Marina. Between 2:00 A.M. and 5:00 A.M. some of the lights got switched off. There was a blanket, her several bundles, and a mat she had unrolled. She wore trousers and a man's padded jacket and was about my age. I lay beside her on the ground. She put a hand between my legs and started to move herself in such a way as to rouse me, which was easy. On the desolate ground near the airport the two of us were on the point of making a glow of pleasure, quietly, one glow perhaps lighting another, and another, making under the blanket our own runway away from pain.

We were smiling. And then we looked into each other's eyes and we saw what had happened. I could do nothing but lie pressed tight against her, swallowing my own saliva. She was still grasping my hard sex in her hand, and her jaw was thrust upwards as if she were trying to kiss with her broken lips something which she could not come close to, her eyes drawn back in slits which pointed to the tips of her ears. When a dog swims, nose in the air, longing for a shore he'll never reach, he has a face like she had lying on the ground beside me. Nothing glows. Everything had been left behind, left with the regular days of the week, the trams she knew, the children's raincoats, her country. Fucking was now a plea for shelter, shelter and nothing else. She let go of me, brushed my ribs gently, and whispered—Ah, man! Forgive me.

Vico's in front, then there's Vica pushing the chariot, and then there's me. We go slowly, like a barge low in the water, but with determination. We are going to the coat in which we live.

The daily howl is diminishing. Towards Ardeatina I hear something else; sounds don't have names and there are as many sounds as words. This one worries me. Maybe it is a silence, an abrupt silence, like the silence following a shot or a yell. The silence of a shock before you feel the pain. I jump into the air, four paws off the ground, and I run. I hear Vica call after me and I ignore her. They can make their own way home and take their time. I'm running towards the coat.

KING

When I get near, I smell diesel oil and spilt water, water spilt onto the dry earth. Not tap water like Vica and I fetch twice a week from the garage. Used water. Dirty water in which pots and clothes have been washed, the washing having been done by men and not women—yes, with my nose I can smell the difference. Let God help me. A lot could explain the water. It's the diesel which frightens me.

Giambattista's theory, Vico explained to me several times, was that all civilizations in this world go through four periods; the periods are long. The first period is the Age of the Gods, when everything is new and everything, even the worst, is possible. Next comes the Age of Heroes, when Helen fucks around in Troy and the Greeks discover the tragic. Afterwards it's the Age of Men, which is the time of politics and sacrifices—no longer for the gods but for human justice. And finally comes the Age of Dogs. After which, says my Vico in his butterfly voice, the cycle will begin again. I ricorsi! I ricorsi! Perhaps he made it up.

I run faster, confused by an explicable fear, and I stop by the Sink. On the far side of the pond I see lights, and they are reflected in the oily surface of the water. The far bank of the little pond looks as straight as the spine of a feather and everything is symmetrical with the silky barbs above and below, and dazzling above and below among the barbs, the same fucking pattern of lights. My gullet where it joins my nose goes dry. There should be no lights there at this hour. The coat buttons up early. At the best there might be a flickering pocket lamp carried by a man going to shit, or Jack the Baron's pumped-up paraffin light visible through his window, for he suffers from insomnia and when he's not sewing a jacket he fills in his lottery forms at night. And what I'm staring at, aghast, are headlights. At least six.

I don't know how late it is. It is dark and I'm lying in the grass on the other side of the river, near the beach where the hermit crabs are. I'm still trembling and I listen to the sea. Maybe the sound of the surf will calm me or render me indifferent. Time will tell. I will describe to you what happened.

The coat lay there in a heap like every night, its folds and hollows and pockets casting deep shadows in the moonlight. What scared me was the military jeep parked where the buckle of the belt would be if the coat had a belt. Its headlights were on although its engine was not running. A searchlight was fixed to its roof. Standing beside the vehicle were four Mobile

Guards with their FAMAS submachine guns. Their officer was sitting in the driving seat of the jeep. He looked as if he was reading.

Yet far worse than the presence of these men and their uniforms was the threat of the massive engine, with its own lights, slowly crossing the terrain from Ostiensis. It moved on caterpillars and I could hear their special raking noise as it advanced. The noise of stones being torn like linen. This machine, painted yellow and black, taller than any lorry that goes to Berlin, is known as the Crawler.

I made for the grass near the right lapel. It was tall enough for me to hide in. I was near enough now to see the officer had a large birthmark, the colour of damsons, on the left side of his neck. He had come down from the jeep and was holding a bullhorn. He wore gloves, and with a gloved hand he made a gesture to one of the guards.

The guard climbed up to switch on the searchlight, and he maneuvered the beam with great deliberation as if he knew what he was looking for, and the beam swept slowly over the coat.

This sweeping was a sign. When it's dark everything is a sign. The guards wanted to show everybody who was hiding that they were going to be swept out.

The officer fiddled with the amplifier of the bullhorn and it made the noise of an intestine grumbling.

The Crawler was getting closer. Its name was written black on yellow: Liebherr. Dear Sir. Its boom was taller than the streetlights along the M.1000. And it could lean and turn and had elbows.

The officer climbed my scrap mountain, the pile from which I survey the terrain, and he lifted the bullhorn to his mouth.

There is no reason for distress, he said. The volume was so high his words were hard to understand.

No reason for distress. We are asking you to come out, all of you. We are inviting you to a hot meal, like you don't often have. A hot meal. We are taking you to better accommodations. Transport is available.

The officer took off one of his gloves to readjust the volume of the amplifier. The Crawler had halted, facing Danny's container.

We are asking you to come out. There is no reason for distress.

With his free hand the officer touched the birthmark on his own neck.

We will be taking you to better accommodations. Tests have been carried out where you are living and they show that the soil is contaminated. There are noxious gases. We insist that you come out.

I saw the face of the driver in the lit cabin of the Crawler. He looked confused. He looked as if he didn't know where to begin. The officer nodded to two guards, saying:

Check there's nobody there, and no animals or gas cylinders.

The two guards approached Danny's place and tore down the blanket—it was a grey one with a red line of little squares at its head and foot—the blanket was hanging over the entrance which Danny had cut out of his container's metal wall. He had used Marcello's acetylene. The opening was narrow because Danny is slim. Vica couldn't step inside, she's too colossal. When Danny told her a joke through the opening, she shook with laughter outside.

A man telephones the police station to tell them his wife is missing. Since when? they ask. Eight days ago, he replies. Then why didn't you inform us before? I thought, says the man, she was talking to the neighbour!

Man's joke! muttered Vica.

Danny never told the same story twice. He collected stories, several a day, as others collect thrown-away yogurts and out-dated bacon.

One of the guards slipped into Danny's container with a torch. Nothing here, Super! he shouted.

Then stand aside!

The Liebherr advanced.

Corinna ran from her van. In the moonlight she looked like a satin slip blown off a clothesline, she was so frail. As she advanced, she swore: Mother-fuckers! Get out of there!

There's nothing left for you to lay your fucking hands on. Get out!

The officer spoke through the bullhorn:

We are asking you all to come out like this good lady has. There is no reason for distress. We are offering you better accommodations. Tests have been carried out which show that living here you are subject to a grave health risk.

Then get out yourself! spat Corinna.

She ran towards the Crawler. God-forbidden beast! she cried and she started to throw stones at it. God-forbidden beast!

The stones were very small and they didn't even hit the grab. She fell to her knees and the driver didn't know what to do. He stopped the engine and sat there in his cabin without moving. What could a man do in his position?

He looked ashamed, and he also looked as if he was going to do what he was ordered to do. He lit a cigarette, and Corinna knelt before the grab. The guards looked towards the officer, waiting for an order. She lifted her hands to the sky, fingers interlaced and imploring. I growled a little to give her courage. The officer indicated she should be taken aside.

A guard came and lifted her to her feet. Come with us, Grandma, he said. You cunts! she screamed. You'll be all right, he said, come along with us and we'll give you something hot to eat.

I have my own wooden chair, she said, and she said these words like a queen.

Then she stooped and by her leg, thin as a post, she picked up a chunk of broken brick and with her right arm turning like the spoke of a chariot wheel threw it high into the air before the guard caught hold of her. The red chunk fell onto the cabin roof of the Crawler. The driver didn't even look up. The guard led her towards the jeep.

I have my own wooden chair, she said again.

The officer beckoned with his finger and the excavator crawled forward. The slowness of the Crawler was like a fearful cramp in your own belly. When you get hit, the blow usually comes so fast you scarcely see it coming. There is the crack and a sudden pain. Violence is usually speedy. The terrible slowness of the Crawler threatened annihilation and its slowness announced there was no escape. I felt myself trembling.

The machine lurched to a standstill. With its boom lowered and probing forward like a gigantic snout, it stretched towards Danny's container. Its crawler tracks were locked. The open jaw of the concrete-crushers, hanging at the end of the snout with its silver pistons, nudged the container and the container edged away. The driver, pale-faced, peered through the unbreakable glass of his cabin window and took a decision. The Crawler raised its head and thumped with its jawbone against Danny's roof. The roof buckled and dented and nothing else moved at all until the last echo of the hollow crash had died away.

Corinna began to weep.

The Crawler lowered its head and the crushers took a bite at one corner of the container, their teeth jagging their way in. Now the Crawler could lift the box up, lift it off the earth, slowly, more slowly than I cared to look at, higher and higher into the darkness, until, crushers opening, it let it fall and hurtle to the ground below.

Another of Danny's jokes: My friend, have you ever seen a man-eating lion? No, but I have seen a man eating herring!

When the container hit the earth and capsized onto its side, nothing rattled in it. It sounded empty. Hopelessly empty.

Danny owned nothing solid except a stolen bicycle which he rode off on each morning. Inside the container, on the metal wall by the mattress on which he slept, he had stuck a photo. The photo was taken by Jack and it showed Luc and Danny and Marcello and Joachim with Catastrophe on Christmas Day last year. Two of them have gone.

Five minutes later, capsized and compressed, Danny's container looked like a hanged man. You could still recognise it, but you could see it had been put to death.

€ € €

The machine was heading now for Alfonso's place. I made a wide circuit, low on the ground, and got there first. Alfonso was sitting on the wooden doorstep in the moonlight where he sometimes leaves a plate for me. I arrived panting. His eyes were shut. This, I knew, was what he was going to do when the Crawler arrived.

He was playing his guitar and he wasn't holding any guitar in his arms. I spotted the guitar case behind the door, lying on the mattress in the room he had built last autumn against the brick wall which was already there. The shiny black case was shut and on the floor there were three empty wine bottles. If I could have got in there, I'd have rolled them with my nose. He had found the floorboards in a deserted dance hall, and he had made five journeys to bring them to Saint Valéry, and he laid them himself and kept them polished.

From far off, a shout rang out. The sea wind was blowing stronger. Again the same shout. I knew it was Jack. It was Jack asking for light. The guards turned the beam towards the collar of the coat, where the shout came from. It showed up Jack standing on top of the tyre dump. In his fist he was holding a large hand bell.

I glanced at Alfonso, whose eyes were still shut. The fingers of his left hand were pressing down on invisible strings, were pressing deliberately, occasionally travelling down over the frets which weren't there. His right hand hovered like a lark, fingers outspread and plucking quickly. Plucking invisible silent pains out of his belly. His foot was beating time. I was frightened, and, like Alfonso, I didn't want to meet what frightened me.

I'm not going to stand for any mucking about, Jack's voice boomed. You could hear Jack without a bullhorn, he had a voice which carried. It didn't carry every word, but it carried the stick of his authority. I forgot my fear for a moment. Alfonso went on tapping with his foot. I slipped away to join the Baron by the tyre dump.

I'm not going to stand for it, not here, shouted Jack. You have no right to touch these shelters when people are living in them, and there are people in every one of them, is that clear? All the shelters are inhabited. Some of them even receive letters! You have been misinformed, Superintendent, we are not going to be flushed out like shit.

The officer was giving instructions to the guards. Hands on their FAMAS, two of them made off in the direction of Alfonso's place.

Do you know, sir, how many people are living in Saint Valéry? shouted the Baron. One hundred and seventeen!

He rang the bell to make the lie truthful. One hundred and seventeen, and every shelter is going to be defended! He rang the bell once more, grim-faced.

There are moments in life when an invented lie is the only thing you have to hang on to—like one of those artificial bones which poor old-age pensioners buy for dogs.

You have been misinformed, sir. You have been given the wrong figures. I will give you a piece of advice. Withdraw now, go back for new orders. I was in the Mayor's office this morning. About face! Comandante, about face!

Hidden in the tyres by the Baron's boot stood a shotgun. Normally it hung on the wall above his bed: a Panther 440 stainless.

On its flank, where you break it to charge it, there was a beautiful engraving in metal of a dog surrounded by roses.

I jumped up onto the tyres to be beside him. When tyres are dumped, they start to smell of the kelp forest. I looked up at him, leaning against his leg. His face was as strong and imperturbable as the radiator of an Iveco lorry. And this frightened me, for I knew about the courage of men like Jack. The nearer they know they are to disaster, the calmer their bearing.

You need daylight, Comandante. You also need a warrant. Call it off for tonight. If you persist, the present situation is going to get out of control, badly out of control. Do you expect me to keep order with a bell? And a bell is all I have!

He jerked the bell up and down, its brass flashing in the searchlight, and he allowed himself to bare his teeth, for this grimace could be explained by his effort; it betrayed nothing more. Then, abruptly, he stopped pumping his arm and he put his other hand inside the bell to silence it. The clapper hurt his fingers.

You need daylight, sir. If the situation flies out of hand tonight I can't answer for it.

He allowed his hand with the bruised fingers to flutter in the air.

You won't be able to answer for it either, sir. And it's you who will be held responsible, isn't that so, King? He dangled his fingers by my nose, and discreetly felt for the top of the barrels of the shotgun with his boot.

I licked his fingers slowly and was off. I had to warn Vico.

Where were they? I opened my mouth and let the night air ruffle my chops and pass a finger lightly along my gums. No message. They were not in the Hut, so where were they? It came to me that there could be another reason why there was no message from the Hut, and I ran away fast from this reason. I ran in the opposite direction, towards the left shoulder of the coat, intending to go down the sleeve.

I passed Anna in her blockhouse.

King, come here! For Christ's sake, over here, King. Where are you running to? King! Stay, stay with me. You'll frighten them, King, if they come up here. They won't dare come in. Pigs are shit-scared, they always are. I can scare one by myself. An old woman like me can scare two of them. But if four come, I'm done for. If four come, two hold me down and the other two do me. Come here, King, I'll give you some meat, I'll open a tin.

I ran on, paws pounding on the voice, pounding on her old woman's voice, her voice thin as a tissue with which they wipe a little child's arse. Madness isn't a wrong path, it's an undergrowth which covers all paths.

By the left armpit Saul was sitting in Luc's Rancho, holding a torch. He had his hat on and the Bible was open on his lap. His knees announced what he was reading.

Because I was not cut off before the darkness, neither has he covered the darkness from my face.

KING

He was sitting on the TV which Marcello had given him. On the ground beside the television, within easy reach, he had placed a butcher's knife, the knife they call a tendon knife. He didn't look up whilst I stood in the doorway.

I ran on farther, paws pounding. I seldom knock into things in the dark. They warn me. They warn me of their position without giving away their real identity or their reason for being there. In the dark I avoided the leaning wooden fence which every day leant nearer to the earth and would soon be a floor. I avoided the two straggling metal frames which were like clothes-dryers large enough to hang bankers' carpets over. I avoided the circular slice of a concrete column, tall as a man, the pebbles on its severed surface coming loose and about to fall out like the white morsels of fat from a stale salami. These strange things were all familiar because they belonged to the place we had made into our coat

I spotted a guard coming up the sleeve. He was making for Marcello's squat, which would be deserted. I veered eastwards and turned right towards Joachim's place . . .

I peered inside the tent. I could see nothing, not even his flashy radio. Blackness. His polyamide sheet was the size and colour of a grey elephant anyway, and tonight he thought it wiser not to light up anything. He was standing there somewhere in the darkness. I could smell his giant's body and his tattoo of Eva and his refusal to fall. I could also smell Catastrophe, his cat, who was in there with him and who was equally invisible. Then I heard him whisper to her:

So you know what's up, don't you? That's why you're dancing a maelstrom in the fucking dark. The gale brushes your whiskers before it gets up, doesn't it? Come here, Catastrophe, come here. You know more than the shipping news, don't you? Force nine, eh, my little pussy? My dry little pussy who doesn't like getting wet. Pussies should like getting wet. It scares you, pussy, abandoning ship. Who likes abandoning ship, who likes it? I ask you. Not a bleeding soul in the world likes it. You sit on my head, little paws in my beard, like that you stay dry. This time we're taking everything strapped onto the raft, everything except the window and door. They can have them. This time those cunts are not going to touch a thing of yours or mine, Catastrophe.

Joachim the Giant talking in the pitch dark to his Catastrophe gave me courage and I changed direction. I retraced my steps as I often do. I would go and see whether the worst had happened. I would face what I feared. Returning to the collar, I went down the right sleeve.

Our Hut was exactly as I had left it that morning. The three mugs were hanging on the inside of the door. The chunks of concrete holding down the plastic sheet were on our roof. The worst had not happened to us.

In the armpit, Liberto and Malak were talking.

They're going to flatten us one by one, she said.

Not if we fight.

They'll force us out.

Not if we fight, Malak, we have no choice. Have you any Tampax?

He's gone out of his mind! King! He's gone out of his mind.

I'm asking you whether you have any Tampax?

What?

I'm asking you.

Almost a packet.

Good. I'll be back immediately.

You won't leave me, don't leave me, Liberto!

Find me three litre bottles. Empty. Glass, not plastic. And I'll be back.

You can't go now.

I'm going up to the Elf garage. We'll need some scraps of rag too. And three Tampax.

Have you seen any empty bottles, King?

I showed her.

Only those also resisting know how my friends resist.

I had to find my honeymoon couple. There was no sign of them on Ardeatina. I returned to the corner from where I'd run off. There I barked. Through a window I watched the flicker of a television. Above the roofs it was getting darker. Clouds swept in from the sea were beginning to mask the moon. Under the roofs elderly couples were already in bed. I barked again, this time calling Vica. And she heard me as she always did. She came out of a bar, a way up the street, and stood at the top of a few steps.

I stayed with my feet on the pavement, looking up at her.

I bought him a whiskey, King. He didn't protest as I thought he would. And do you know what he said, King? You've forgiven me, he said. And me? I said, Forgive me! I said.

Quick, I panted, both of you, quick.

Let him finish his whiskey, King. He hasn't eaten all day, and he's happy.

We don't have time.

Nobody's going to lock us out, we're going to sleep in our bed, like we do every night. I have a secret to tell you, come here.

I went up the steps to fetch her.

Don't you want to hear my secret? I'll whisper it in your ear.

Not now. Get Vico.

It's a secret I have to tell you alone.

Quick!

Why quick? It took me years to see what I want to tell you.

KING

They're going to flatten us! I told her brutally.

Us?

Where we live.

Not at this time of night. What have you been sniffing, King?

Go to the corner of the street, I said, and you'll see the lights which shouldn't be there. Go home and I'll fetch Vico.

When I pushed open the door, I recognized the kind of bar it was.

Women are rare in these bars and there's never a barmaid. A narrow little local bar where the clock stops some time after 10:00 P.M. The men standing at the counter have missed out on supper, so there's no pressing reason for them to go home, although they live round the corner. They are there most nights. They know some of each other's secrets and they're experts in silence, even when they slur their words. When the clock stops, nobody orders again, yet they delay leaving, for here in the narrow bar they are recognised and they remain unbetrayed, and there is a warmth in that. The secret they all share and want to forget is why they don't go home. For each one it's different and for each one the consequence is the same. During two years of my life I spent my evenings in such a bar.

As soon as the door slammed behind me, the three men standing by the counter turned their heads.

Hey, boy! they said as if they knew I was one of them.

I walked past. Vico was sitting alone at a table in the corner. He was holding a tumbler in both hands and sniffing the whiskey left in it with his head lowered. Like this he looked as if he was on the point of lapping it up with his tongue—like an animal without hands does. He was smiling. He didn't see me until I touched his knee.

So you've come to fetch me.

I nodded.

Vica bought me a whiskey. She said I deserved it.

We need to get home, I said.

What's the hurry?

They've come.

At this time of night?

They're carting us off. They're smashing everything. They've smashed Danny's place and Marcello's and probably they're smashing Alfonso's now.

Alfonso isn't there?

He lost heart, so he lost everything. All he did was shut his eyes. If we're there, they won't dare, they'll back off. The Baron has warned them. He's got a gun. If we're there, they'll back off.

Where are they carting people to?

Somewhere to be relodged, they say.

Do you know what Giambattista wrote?

You've told me everything he wrote! I replied, exasperated.

I once asked Liberto, who reads a lot, whether he had heard of Vico. Vico? he replied. Never. Rulfo, yes, but not Vico.

Listen to this, Vico said, finishing off his glass of whiskey: "I find very improbable Aristotle's notion that bodies are made up of geometric points. How can one make real things out of abstractions?" That's what Giambattista said. None of us is going to be relodged in reality, King. Everything they tell us is abstraction. Reality is—

Where's the chariot? I interrupted.

It's out at the back, I hid it there. Bring one of those chariots into a bar and they won't serve you, they point to the door. It's no more the Age of Heroes, King, not any more the time of Orestes

Fetch it, man, and run!

It was the only time I ever snapped at him.

Somehow we managed it across Ardeatina, the three of us, and started our trek across the terrain. It was like fighting a blizzard, all our movements were slowed down, as if no action could attain its end. It wasn't cold. The gusts of wind were ferocious now, blowing dust and sand against our noses and chests. And although there was still moonlight, the two of them couldn't see where they were putting their feet and the ground was full of pitfalls. Neither of them could steer the chariot. It kept blocking, lurching, falling.

We'll have to abandon it, said Vico breathlessly, we'll fetch it in the morning.

If we leave it here, it may go, said Vica.

Not if I fetch it early, before it's light, before anyone is up. King and I, we'll fetch it home tomorrow.

Vico's reference to the next morning reassured them, and they abandoned the chariot.

Hold on to me, and I placed myself between them, Vica on my left, Vico on the right.

They grasped me and I led them firmly along a path I could see between the tips, the diggings, the falling banks, the holes full of water, and the smashed cathode ray tubes. It's my gift to follow unmarked, untrodden paths. Vico's hand, warm and scaly, was relaxed on my neck; I must have imparted some confidence to him. Vica, with her swollen fingers, occasionally scratched with one nail the back of my head, as she did when we were lying down.

I wanted to stop to mark that moment. With their hands on me, I forgot my fear. Trusting my nose, the two of them thought they knew where we were going. I paused so briefly to mark the moment of confidence that neither of them noticed. A little later

Vica announced, whistling through her lips: King's leading us home.

❦ ❦ ❦

When we eventually reached the Sink, the Crawler was nowhere to be seen. Its driver was discussing with the officer in front of the jeep, and the two men appeared to be arguing. The guards were standing around, bored with waiting. One of them climbed onto the jeep and swept the coat with the searchlight. Then he switched off, jumped with both feet together, and measured the distance on the ground he'd jumped; he was that bored. The beam had revealed where the Crawler was. It was parked behind the scrap mountain, and its stick was taller than the mountain.

The three of us, running and stumbling, saw at the same moment what had been done. There was no Hut. The Hut had been scattered, compressed, split, leveled, and left there. Even bombardments—and I have seen a number—don't wipe out like this, for then the terrible destruction comes in a flash from the sky. Here the wiping-out had been slow, blind, and close-up.

Vica flung herself onto the wreckage face down. She crawled forward several times, rucking up one leg of her jeans. Under the swelling of her calf I saw a scratch of blood and I listened to her heart breaking. Take the letter V and snap both sticks ʼ✓˥. This is what had happened to her.

I sat beside her. Vico nodded and said, Wait there. Then he turned his back and walked slowly towards the jeep.

I didn't lick her or touch her. I just breathed so that she should know I was there. Under the buried, twisted bed frames of the walls, and the smashed polystyrene, I could make out where the cast-iron stove had been. Without stirring from her side, I searched for a fragment of the bottling jar. My nostrils were quivering. I thought I spotted a shred of the red rubber washer. Then I heard Vico's voice:

We are being wiped off the earth, not the face of the earth, the face we lost long ago, the arse of the earth, *il culo*. We are their mistake, King, listen to me!

I watched him walking. In the jeep headlights every detail about him was cut and dried. The sleeves of his jacket hung loose. His white hair was standing on end. He had one arm raised like a man waving a stick at somebody running away.

A mistake, King, is hated more than an enemy. Mistakes don't surrender as enemies do. There's no such thing as a defeated mistake. Mistakes either exist or they don't, and if they do, they have to be covered over. We are their mistake, King. Never forget that.

Vico's walk had changed; suddenly there was nothing shuffling about his steps. He was walking with decision, and he was light on his toes, almost as if dancing. There was no music to be heard, and the shoulders of his jacket were misshapen and broken. I told all this to Vica, and I don't know if she heard me or understood me.

KING

The officer had spotted Vico, and with his gloved hand he made a sign of acknowledgement. He would ask the old derelict to say a few words to the others through the bullhorn, to tell them to come out as he had had the good sense to do. He looked at his watch to check the late hour.

Perhaps it was the glare of the headlights which made it difficult to judge distances or time. Vico was walking decisively towards the jeep, yet the time he took to cover the distance seemed very long. All the things which were watching him noticed this. Everything had the impression that the piles of muck and the stones and the dumped machine parts, as soon as he had passed them, moved of their own accord and put themselves in front of him again.

Humare, King, the Latin word for "to bury," has gone under. The new word is demolish. Demolish, demolition, gone. Demolish so there's nothing to be seen. Like you can no longer see the stars Vica painted on the wall.

Vica did not move. I laid my head on her back. There was sand on the nape of her neck, the nape which, despite herself, used to smile when she was pleased. Pressing my ear against her hard, I listened. Faintly I heard the beat of a smashed Hut under her shoulder blade. She gave no sign of knowing. The swollen fingers of her left hand twitched and curled up. I pushed my wet nose into her hand.

King, can you hear me?

I sprang up, legs tensed. The officer was holding out the bullhorn to Vico and saying: Please tell your friends, sir, to come out.

Giambattista saw it coming, King.

I ran faster than I ever ran towards Vico.

He didn't have the words and he didn't know the pain, King. He spent his life grappling with the riddle of exactly how and by what stages man had emerged from barbarism. This was his New Science, what he called history. He foresaw a second barbarism, King, which is worse than the first. The first barbarism, according to him, had a certain generosity to it. A strange word to use, isn't it, yet he used it. It was generous because it affected only man's senses. The second barbarism is implanted not in the senses but in thought itself, and this makes it far more vile and far more cruel. The second barbarism kills a man and takes everything whilst it promises and talks of freedom.

We want everything wrapped up as soon as possible, the officer said.

Vico's smashed face was impassive. He held his left hand in the air and it made the gesture of turning over a page. His right hand was hidden behind his back. In it he was clutching his bone-handled knife. After years of use a hand comes to know a knife and a knife recognises its hand. His wrecked face still impassive, he lifted his arm and plunged fist and knife downwards towards the officer's belly.

It can happen that the old do things which nobody else will.

The next instant Vico lay crumpled on the earth. There was blood on the knife which had fallen to the ground. I don't know whose blood. The officer rubbed his knee gently, the knee of the leg whose kick had just felled the old man who was my master. A guard, submachine gun unslung and pointing at his head face down on the ground, stood over him.

Vico knew where I was. I was watching him between the guard's boots. Vai da Vica, he said.

I obeyed him, and on my way I came upon Liberto and Malak huddled together near the Crawler.

I want you out of the way, King, and quick, and I want you out of the way too, Malak.

I could light it and you throw it, she whispered.

Never. If you're here, I worry.

I'll hold the torch, she coaxed.

It's a three-second job, and there's no time for worry. It has to be done clean, which means alone.

What do you want? she asked.

Back at home and wait for me. I'll be there.

Ciao.

Wait, give me your lighter.

Liberto—I couldn't live without you.

I'll give you one minute, he said.

Vica had not moved. The fingers of her hand were curled up. She was lying face down like Vico was.

The two of them face down on the earth, two hundred metres apart.

When Liberto threw his cocktail against the Crawler, I heard air being sucked up by flames and instantly spat out. It was like a sob, an explosive sob.

All around, voices started shouting and it was easy to distinguish between them. The difference between the weak and the strong should not be so clear. The cries from the coat were anxious, furious, insistent; the shouts of the guards were relieved and jubilant because the waiting was over, the mission would soon be accomplished, and they would get home to bed, perhaps to fuck.

€ € €

Vica did not raise her head or move her body. Only her swollen hand searched in the dust near her shoulder, as a sleeper's hand sometimes searches for a nose rag under a bundle. I licked her leg. Her leg was cold, too cold. I ran off to Jack's place to find a blanket or covering for her.

Near the tyre dump Jack had built himself a fortress. He had constructed a tower of the largest tyres, rear-tractor-wheel-size, one on top of the other, and had climbed into them so they surrounded him. When he squatted he was protected and invisible. When he stood up he could rest his elbow on the top one, take aim, and fire. Eight cartridges, I had time to count them: three red ones for wild boar, five yellow ones for game birds, were arranged in a row along the wall of the top tyre. His Panther, I guess, was charged with two red cartridges.

He was standing up, gun across his chest, eyes skinned to scan the terrain and to pick out the slightest movement. Slowly he turned, revolved in a full circle, like a lighthouse, ready to defend his own against any and every comer. It took him about a minute to make the full circle.

The agonizing varieties, Agamemnon, of a common fate.

How many minutes did I watch him? Once he readjusted the sock-cap on his head. The thumb of his right hand remaining on the safety catch.

Before I could shut my mouth, before I felt a rising in my chest, I was howling, head thrown back at the stars.

Who and what survives destruction can only make a story in another life.

It was the helplessness, the solitude, and the finality of this truth which made me howl.

Here, King, here!

Who survives why, Baron? Who and why?

What's up? Where's your Vica? Where's her husband? So they flushed you out, eh? I warned you, didn't I? You have to be there—bloody there—if you want to defend your own.

He kissed his gun without a smile.

We are their mistake, the dog said.

Where's Vico? Shit! Are you sure?

The Baron and the dog looked at one another. Then the Baron scanned the terrain again.

You need balls to do what Vico did, he said eventually.

His real name's Gianni, the dog told him.

Fetch her, the Baron said, she can stay under my roof, go and fetch her.

A shot rang out. A rifle from near the belt of the coat. The Baron narrowed his eyes and instantly brought his own gun to the shoulder. The sea wind blew into our faces. Nothing else moved amongst the ground shadows. He steadied his left elbow on the topmost tyre.

I respect the reflexes of old soldiers. What I hate are bullhorns.

Another shot, and this time our ears heard a whir, a sound of propulsion, the noise of something that cannot be pulled back.

The Baron looked up into the sky, the sky in which, according to Vico, there was no such thing as the constellation of the

Mule. I followed the Baron's gaze and saw two dirty pillows slit open and from them smoking fibres fluttering downwards. A third shot. The pillows were the colour of the Swedish army overcoat.

Tear gas, announced Jack very quietly.

The stuffing from the pillows was becoming a cloud.

A wet rag, the Baron instructed, tie a wet rag across the nose and mouth. Warn them, King, warn them quick. Not nylon, use either cotton or wool—wet rags!

The Baron pulled off his sock-cap, wet it in a tyre in which rain had collected, nicked its knitted crown with a knife, and tugged it over his face to cover it. The wind may help, he added, and the ground's dry for Christ's sake so it'll rise soon, for Christ's sake keep low, keep low as you can, quick, go and warn them. I'll look after the mistress.

The dog, as he ran off, told the Baron the barbarism of today grabs everything across the world whilst it promises promises and talks of freedom.

I kept to the cloud's edge. Everyone heard my warning. The gas was as sinister as the Crawler, the silence of the gas as sinister as the Crawler's slowness. Soundlessly it was turning air into enemy.

Poison is lazy. It pushes the body which it attacks to self-destruction. It operates like despair. Despair is a poison too. The frenetic energy comes from the victim.

The chlorine in the tear gas requires contact with moisture, with water, in order to produce the bleach of sodium chloride. And so, the moist eyes of Anna as she peered out of her blockhouse were forced to collaborate in their own blinding, and the bleach stung her eyeballs so sharply she rubbed her eyes fiercely with her fists and the sodium chloride penetrated further to attack her eustachian tubes. Whereupon she fell to her knees with the pain, and crawled out of the blockhouse towards the collar, where the cloud seemed less thick.

Watching the old woman who had begged me to stay with her, and remembering the bullhorn and feeling the first razor irritation in my own eyes, I wanted to ask Vico whether laziness was not the mother and father of all cowardice. Vico thought himself a coward and he wasn't. I ran through the darkness barking his name: Vico! Vico! In places gusts of wind swirled into the soiling gas and tore it into dirty veils which drifted upwards. Vico! Then, muffled yet distinct, I heard his voice, his butterfly voice in the poisonous air: I ricorsi, King! I ricorsi!

In places the wind folded the gas, thinning it here and doubling it there, and in one of the clearings I thought I recognised the coat's right pocket, only Joachim's place had vanished. There was no tent of polyamide the size of an elephant. There was no joke of a notice board hammered into the earth, saying: BUILDING SITE—KEEP OUT. There was only a door laid carefully on the ground and a window placed on top of it. The home had gone, and yet there was no trace of the Crawler. The Crawler leaves traces.

The wind folded the gas again and I saw a pile. The polyamide sheeting rolled and tied up with a sailor's knot, a gas cylinder, two plastic buckets, the smallest possible machine for making espresso coffee, the flashing radio of which Joachim is so proud, and a four-wheeled pram. Nearby, the man was crawling on all fours, with Catastrophe tucked into his leather jacket. This giant of a man on his hands and knees was retching, like a child who doesn't know how to vomit properly.

Tear gas contains vanolo nitrite, a constricting agent. The salt of nitric acid irritates the windpipe so that it tries to close, beginning at the larynx and going down to the bronchial tubes, provoking a fear of suffocation. Since he was a giant, the reactions of Joachim's body were particularly violent. He had no idea where he was. I tugged at him and led him towards the collar. More or less blindly we made it to where we could breathe a little more easily. We lay close to the earth. Through the darkness, distantly, we could hear the bullhorn:

Disperse towards the M.1000, the air is clear there and you will be led to the transport which has been waiting for you. Do not delay any more. We are asking you this in your—

The message broke off because the Baron had fired one of his wild boar cartridges. After one minute's total silence the bullhorn yelled: So you are asking for it—are you?

This is the most common phrase which precedes torture, rape, or killing. That much I know. On this occasion it announced the last clumsy phase of an ill-organised operation for the flushing out of illegal squatters from land which had been bought for investment. I could still smell sulphur and ammonia. I asked myself where I should take the giant, who was still blind and occasionally whooping. The idea came to me like a homing scent. I would take him to the Boeing. It was not more than three hundred metres away. We would have to skirt numerous thickets of gas, and they were visible and I would lead him. At one moment I told him to ride on me as if I was a mule. And he did, with his feet touching the ground, and I was strong enough to carry him.

Out of a gas thicket stumbled Saul, his arms held out in front of him so as not to collide with the devil, and his face bleeding. Both men were too prudent about opening their mouths to say a word. They looked towards me and their eyes were screwed up. The Boeing lay towards the sea, from which the wind was blowing, and it was in a hollow and the gas was rising because the ground was dry, so I persisted. Normally I might have had many doubts. Tonight, the pain of the giant and of the retired slaughterer was so close-up that there was no space for doubt. If I had left them where we were, they would have survived—yet a strange half-thought came to me that if we reached the Boeing we would go somewhere better.

We pressed on and caught up with Alfonso, who had his hat over his face and the guitar case on his back. The giant dismounted from my back and the singer supported him with one arm. Still nobody said a word. The three men I was leading were as silent as shadows are invisible in the total dark.

If I hadn't been leading they would have tripped over Anna, prostrate on the ground in her black coat.

No time to die, and I nipped her ear.

Going to kill, she wheezed.

Get up! I said.

Strangle one tonight, she said.

I didn't tell her about Vico. I pushed her ahead.

At last we reached the Boeing. The four of them slid down the slope on their arses, by a common accord, by an instinct for survival. The air was pure down there and it was very dark. Clouds hid the moon. Malak and Liberto had had the same idea and were already installed. They hadn't taken off the rag masks they were wearing according to the Baron's instructions. Nobody spoke. No longer because they had to be prudent about breathing in air, but because when everything has been lost, time stops for a while, and talking needs time.

Time had stopped for me, which is why I lay there panting instead of going straightaway to find Vica. And again the strange half-thought came to me that we could go, all of us, Vica included, to somewhere better.

Any of you down there in the Boeing 747? It was Danny's voice from above.

Yes, said Malak.

Danny flicked his lighter alight and picked his way down. He looked in good shape and must have somehow avoided the tear gas.

Have you heard this one? he asked.

Silence.

None of you heard this one?

He lay down where the others were sprawling.

A man comes up to the driver of a car which has stopped at a traffic light and says, very agitated: Sir, your car is smoking! Really, says the driver, what brand?

You saw your place? Liberto asked Danny.

I saw it, said Danny.

This was the last word said. The seven of them waited, hidden in the Boeing, sprawled on the earth. I don't know why they waited. It was pitch dark. The Liebherr had performed more than half its task. The guards would soon be searching. The bus was there to take them away and to separate them. Their eyes were burning. They waited because they did not know where to go. They were breathing easily. The next breath was assured. Beyond the next breath they did not know where to go. So they waited.

They were aware of each other, and in the Boeing this was better than being alone. They did not know where to go. Anna spat loudly. Joachim started coughing. Danny began to shiver, his teeth chattering. Malak put her shawl over him. Saul cleared his throat several times as if about to speak. Joachim's cough became drier and drier, like a bark. This made me bark.

A bark is a voice which breaks out of a bottle saying: I'm here. The bottle is silence. The silence broken, the bark announces: I'm here.

Joachim's cough barked again. Alfonso barked. The bark of another one prods your ears, presses on your tongue, and forces the jaw to open in reply: I'm here! Saul barked, throwing out the diabolic gas he'd swallowed. Malak barked, twisting the ring on her finger. They did not know where to go. They were like me. Liberto barked. They were like me.

After a while you forget you're barking, and when this happens you hear the others, you hear the chorus of barks and, although not one of them has changed and each is distinct, so distinct that it can break a heart, the barking is saying something different now, it's saying: We're here! and this *we're here* blows on an almost dead memory, and it revives like the dead ashes of a fire glowing again thanks to a night wind, and the memory is of the pack, of fear, of the forest, and of food.

They were barking as they lay there and I listened to the names of their barks: Danny the terrier, Joachim, Saul, Malak, Anna, Alfonso, Liberto the spitz. Crouched in the dust bowl of the Boeing, they had nothing, like I had nothing. We were the same, and we were all barking.

It being the first time, it seemed better I lead them and set the pace. The moon was hidden behind rags of invisible clouds and the night was black. They would follow because they would be packed together, touching, noses against flanks, ears flicked by a tail, a trail of dust in the blackness left behind. They would follow.

We scrambled out of the Boeing, and I headed for the collar to find Jack and Vica. The two of them must have heard us calling long before we arrived, for they were ready by the tyre dump, waiting.

Vica, colossal xolo, little dog from the Sierra Madre, with your truffle nose and tight eyelids, come and run beside me. It was the xolos, my love, who led the Aztec dead to their hereafters.

Near a city in the small hours of the morning a wild pack of running barking dogs is unnerving. A single spray from a FAMAS would be enough to dispatch the lot and leave most moaning in agony on the ground. Yet the ancestral memory of the apparition goes so far back that the guard forgets he has a submachine gun.

By the time he remembered and slipped the FAMAS off his shoulder, Corinna and Vico had joined us and we had swerved sharply east, so the guard was firing blindly into the blackness where there was nobody and nothing.

Vico, our midget deer hunter.

Corinna, thin as a rake, who doesn't eat, Corinna, who never ate when young on heroin, Corinna, the saluki with the longest nose, whose tip was turned up as she ran, as if she were smiling instead of sniffing glue.

Jack the Great Dane.

I was leading them to the sea by the shortcut. We cantered slowly. We were out of danger. The rhythm of their paws pounding the earth together lightened their fatigue. To their own music even the old can dance all night.

Their different-sized feet, their delicate cannon bones, their elbows pushed wasteland after wasteland away, and with each stride the leap into the air was a little more sure and the landing on the earth a little briefer, so the air became like a music which carried them. The sky was so dark it lay cheek to cheek with the rubble and scoria, and the darkness laid its hands on their flanks and rumps so the pack lost its suffering memory and only listened to the rap of its own fury and appetite.

Our tongues were hanging out to get rid of the salt of our sweat.

All this I believed until we reached the river and the bridge covered with grass from which everything slopes down to the sea. From the hump of this bridge I looked back for the first time and found there was nobody behind me. I had fled alone from the Boeing.

Liberto, Malak, Jack, Corinna, Danny, Anna, Joachim, Saul, Alfonso, Vica, and Vico, the deer hunter, are still there sheltering in what remains of the coat.

The duplicity of words. No, I correct myself again. Every third one at least comes from the heart.

These I found on the marble floor by the font in the Church of Santa Maria on the hill.

> The china font of holy water
> above the china bowl

with open arms
the china Christ
no taller than a finger
and the maker's full brush of blue
tracing down the left side
the length of his robe
dark as blood
blue as prayer

I'm lying in the grass on the other side of the river and I don't know how late it is.

You Vica, you darling, were blue as prayer.

There are no arms to lie in.

This story was
written by John Berger, who
would like to thank for their help,
encouragement, and belief, Aline, Anders,
André, Anne, Beverly, Bobo, Erica, Geoff, Ghislaine,
Gianni, Giovanni, Hans, Hervé, Jana, Jane, Jean-Jacques,
Juan, Katya, Latife, Lilo, Marc, Maria, Maria,
Marisa, Martin, Michael, Miquel, Nella,
Nikos, Pilar, Riccardo, Robert, Ronald,
Rostia, Sandra, Simon, Tim,
Witek, Yves, Yvonne

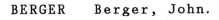